M000166362

©lack

Ugly and selfish—you've heard stories about these creatures. There's no question what you're dealing with. *Goblins!*

Here in the fortress city, it was not particularly unusual to see adventurers playing cards in the tavern.

A party of adventurers who had been sitting around a table in the morning wouldn't come back that night. The table would still be empty the next morning, and the day after that, a different party with brand-new equipment would fill the seats. That, too, was just how life went here in the fortress city.

CONTENTS

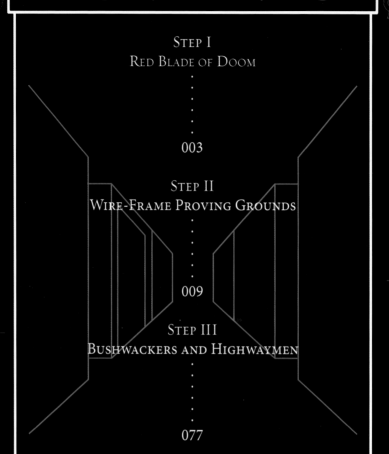

DAI KATANA

The Singing Death

GOBLIN SLAYER
SIDE STORY II

DAI KATANA
The Singing Death

KUMO KAGYU
ILLUSTRATION BY lack

YEN
ON
NEW YORK

GOBLIN SLAYER
SIDE STORY II
DAI KATANA
The Singing Death

KUMO KAGYU **1** ILLUSTRATION BY lack

Translation by Kevin Steinbach ✦ Cover art by lack

This book is a work of fiction. Names, characters, places, and incidents are the product of the author's imagination or are used fictitiously. Any resemblance to actual events, locales, or persons, living or dead, is coincidental.

GOBLIN SLAYER GAIDEN 2: DAI KATANA Volume 1
Copyright © 2019 Kumo Kagyu
Illustrations copyright © 2019 lack
All rights reserved.
Original Japanese edition published in 2019 by SB Creative Corp.
This English edition is published by arrangement with SB Creative Corp., Tokyo in care of
Tuttle-Mori Agency, Inc., Tokyo.

English translation © 2020 by Yen Press, LLC

Yen On
150 West 30th Street, 19th Floor, New York, NY 10001

Visit us at yenpress.com • facebook.com/yenpress • twitter.com/yenpress
yenpress.tumblr.com • instagram.com/yenpress

First Yen On Edition: December 2020

Yen On is an imprint of Yen Press, LLC.
The Yen On name and logo are trademarks of Yen Press, LLC.

The publisher is not responsible for websites (or their content) that are not owned by the publisher.

Library of Congress Cataloging-in-Publication Data
Names: Kagyū, Kumo, author. | lack (Illustrator), illustrator.
Title: Goblin Slayer side story II: dai katana / Kumo Kagyu ; illustration by lack.
Other titles: Goblin Slayer gaiden 2: tsubanari no daikatana. English
Description: First Yen On edition. | New York : Yen On, 2020–
Identifiers: LCCN 2020043585 | ISBN 9781975318239 (v. 1 ; trade paperback)
Subjects: LCSH: Goblins—Fiction. | GSAFD: Fantasy fiction.
Classification: LCC PL872.5.A367 G5313 2020 | DDC 895.63/6—dc23
LC record available at https://lccn.loc.gov/2020043585

ISBNs: 978-1-9753-1823-9 (paperback)
978-1-9753-1824-6 (ebook)

1 3 5 7 9 10 8 6 4 2

LSC-C

Printed in the United States of America

GOBLIN SLAYER
SIDE STORY II

DAI KATANA

The Singing Death

Characters

YOU
G-SAM
HUMAN MALE

At the entrance to the Dungeon of the Dead in the northern reaches of the Four-Cornered World, there is a fortress city. A human adventurer has just arrived there. He is a warrior who has mastered the ways of the sword.

FEMALE WARRIOR
N-FIG
HUMAN FEMALE

A girl you meet in the fortress city. An "old hand," she's already been down in the dungeon. A human warrior who wields a spear.

FEMALE BISHOP
G-BIS
HUMAN FEMALE

A girl you meet at the tavern in the fortress city. She lost her eyes on a previous adventure. She can identify items by the power of the Supreme God.

DAIKATANA: The Singing Death

One of the All-Stars	Hawkwind	Elite Solar Trooper, Special Agent, and Four-Armed Humanoid Warrior Ant

COUSIN
G-MAG
HUMAN FEMALE

Your older cousin, who accompanied you to the fortress city. She's a kind woman who looks after you like a sister would, but sometimes you think she's not all there. A human wizard, she supports you from the back row.

HALF-ELF SCOUT
N-THI
HALF-ELF MALE

An adventurer you met on your way to the fortress city. As entertaining as he is keen-eyed, he serves as your party's scout.

MYRMIDON MONK
G-PRI
MYRMIDON MALE

An adventurer you met in the fortress city. An old hand in the dungeon, he serves as your party's strategist. He is a Myrmidon or "Bugman Monk" who serves the Trade God.

Those who knew how it began were no more.

Perhaps some unfortunate farmer moved a stone that should have stayed put. Maybe some foolish child undid a seal in a shrine somewhere. It may have even been a fiery stone shooting across the heavens.

Whatever the cause, it was not so very long ago that the Death began stalking the continent.

Disease traveled on the wind, consuming all the people it encountered; the dead rose, the trees withered, the air grew foul and the water rancid.

The King of Time issued a proclamation: "Find the source of this Death and seal it away."

Thus heroes arose all over the continent, and so they, too, were swallowed one by one by the Death, leaving nothing but their corpses.

The only exception was a single party, which left these words alone: "The maw of the Death lies in the northernmost reaches."

None left knew who discovered this. For those adventurers, too, were spirited away by the Death.

The Dungeon of the Dead.

The entrance to this vast abyss yawned like the jaws of the Reaper, and people gathered at the foot of it, until finally a fortress city was born.

In this city, adventurers sought companions, challenged the dungeon, battled, found loot…and sometimes died.

These days of glory went on, and on, and on, repeating over and over.

Riches and monsters welled up without end—as did the incessant hack and slash.

Life was spilled like so much water as adventurers drowned in their own dreams until the fire disappeared from their eyes.

Sooner or later, all that remained, glowing like an ember, were the ashen days of adventuring, which went hand in hand with the Death…

RED BLADE OF DOOM

The light is faster than the sound: A red blade slices past your eyeballs, followed by a belated *whoosh*. One half of a dungeon tile. That's how narrowly you avoided death, just a shuffle of your feet.

You react immediately, closing in and bringing your katana up in a diagonal strike. There's a ringing of metal, and you feel a dull numbness in your hands. The sword bounces back. You were too slow, frustratingly slow.

Grasping the hilt, you sling your beloved weapon over your shoulder. No follow-up attack comes.

You see just the ghost of a smile in the dim light. It's laughing at you. Well, let it laugh.

"Hey, you, over here…!"

A spear comes stabbing in from the side. The voice seems so soft for one with a weapon so sharp. It's a female warrior. The two of you no longer need words to coordinate your actions. But that doesn't make you infallible.

"Hrrr-agh?!"

Another red flash cuts through the darkness, and again the sound comes late, a clash of steel. Sparks fly, and the spear is deflected. Now the red blade describes a great upward arc. A strike from above. Her face tenses, anticipating the blow. But then—

"Whoa—!"

Parried.

A half-elf scout, holding a butterfly-shaped dagger in a reverse grip, just manages to push the blade off its path. Female Warrior smiles at him as best she can, in acknowledgment of his fine, light-footed entrance. Spear in hand, she struggles to get back to her feet. "Sorry, that one's on me."

"All good, but…I can't handle this one alone!"

With each flash of red light, Half-Elf Scout's body sports fresh wounds. He's a scout, after all. One-on-one combat isn't his calling. *I could use a little help here*, he seems to be saying.

When you ask if she can stand, Female Warrior says, "I'll try." Good.

You advance once more, your sword still across your shoulder, charging straight ahead and swinging three times. But the red blade blocks each cut, sweeping your attacks aside and always moving ever backward as smoothly as if it were melting away. Then, suddenly, you feel a chill down your spine and jump back. The blade flashes through the space where your neck had been an instant before.

That would have been a critical hit!

"This sucks—it's six-on-one, and we can barely hold on! It don't make any sense!"

You agree with Half-Elf Scout. You would certainly like to settle this if you could.

There's an exclamation from behind you: "It's worse than that—look!" Myrmidon Monk sounds unusually agitated. It doesn't take you long to figure out why. Something is bubbling up from the darkness—or rather, somethings.

"GHOOOOOOOOOOULLLLL!!"

"GGGGGGGHOOOULL…!"

Red eyes, pale, dead flesh grotesquely swollen. Dressed in rags and flashing fanged mouths, they must be vampires. Nightwalkers, nightwalkers, nightwalkers! And a great many of them, as if every adventurer to die in these depths has been summoned back from the grave. You have no idea how many of them might wait in the dark of this unknowable expanse.

"So much for six-on-one. Think your numbers were a little off,"

Myrmidon Monk says, his antennae bobbing vigilantly. He clacks his mandibles together. "Though it makes no difference to our plan—to kill them all. We and they have that much in common, at least."

"Well, there goes complaining about how we can't win despite the advantage in numbers," Female Warrior says. "Now they've got the numbers, and they're some tough customers." *Not fair at all.*

Your face is tight as you nod at Female Warrior, then ready your sword in a low stance. You slide forward, taking care to not lift your feet as you close the distance to your opponents, trying to find their presence. Where is the red blade? You can't make out even the silhouettes of your foes in the darkness. The idea of being able to sense an enemy's presence is a rather nebulous one anyway. Honestly, there probably is no such thing. There's only sound, the rasping of breath, traces of body heat, eddies in the air. The five senses tell all there is to tell.

Female Warrior looks at you, and you can feel the trust her eyes convey. She seems to have noticed how calm your breathing is.

"So," she says, "what's the plan?"

The edges of your lips curl up as you tell her that there is only ever one plan. Destroy each and every one of them.

Heh: She gives a good-natured shrug, her pale face breaking into a smile. It seems you've successfully relieved the tension.

"Mm." Myrmidon Monk grunts thoughtfully. "Would you like me to switch to the front row? I don't mind either way."

"Get outta town!" Half-Elf Scout says, despite the cold sweat drenching him. "Only one of us can chop off that bastard's head, and it's gonna be me!"

"Excellent!" Myrmidon Monk laughs, clacking his mandibles approvingly at the scout's show of enthusiasm. At the same time, he works his knotty fingers, tracing a complicated sigil. The Seal of Return.

"There's a good chance these undead are weak to Dispel…!" The one who calls out is the party's female wizard, your cousin who's incidentally also charged with resource management. "Three moves after Dispel! Let's do it! Coordinate with me!"

"Right!" comes the eager voice of the bishop beside your cousin, holding the sword and scales. The light has long since gone out of her eyes, which are covered by a bandage, yet her gaze contains the utmost resolution. She was weak once, but now she is a seasoned adventurer.

Even as you marvel at the bishop's growth, you grunt your own acknowledgment of your cousin's instructions, tracing a sigil with your free hand.

"O my god of the wind that comes and goes, send home these souls!"

Opening gambit: Myrmidon Monk's Dispel fills the space with a fresh, violent wind.

Ashes to ashes, dust to dust. The rotting corpses are unable to withstand this purifying air, akin as it is to the Resurrection miracle that restores life. The legions of restless dead in this dungeon were not summoned by a curse, but before a high-level miracle, they succumb just the same.

As the nightwalkers crumble into dust, your cousin's voice sounds loudly: "*Ventus!* Wind!"

"*Lumen!* Light!" continues Female Bishop. She brandishes the sword and scales, intoning the words of the spell as if delivering a proclamation from her god.

The words of magic invoked by the two women overwrite the very logic of the world, refashioning it and producing immense power. The wind turns to a gale, and even your eyes can perceive the light condensing.

And finally, you, too, speak a word of true power, unleashing it all with the sigil formed by your hand.

'Libero! *Release!*'

A storm of wind.

Blinding light.

Roaring noise.

And heat.

The grave-dark room, having nearly become an alternate dimension, is flooded with piercing light. Those undead who escaped the effects of Dispel now scream as their flesh boils away. There is nothing in the world that can flee Fusion Blast.

"Captain—!"

"Oh crap…!"

At least, not if it is *of* this world.

You are lucky. In response to your friends' shouts, you dodge, rolling along the stone floor. The red blade flashes before you, and there is a spray of blood. The spray is accompanied by a whistling sound. Like a rain of crimson, it spills from the throat of Female Warrior, right in front of your eyes.

"Hhh—rrr...ahhh?!" She presses her hands against her neck, her face bloodless, before she collapses to her knees. The red blade slides through the air again. Overhead in a grim repeat of last time. It's moments away from decapitating her.

"You—son of a—!" Half-Elf Scout shoves the blow aside. But the butterfly-shaped blade is smacked away, once, twice, and then his abdomen opens. "What the—? Hrrrgh—?!"

You can hear the blade bury itself deep in his bowels. Blood comes pouring from the scout's mouth. With your companions fallen before you, you grip your blade and rise to your feet. That was two of them.

"...!" Your cousin speaks quickly: "They need healing! You focus on the front row; I'll worry about the back!" You've always respected the way she keeps her cool in even the most extreme situations. And so, even as your companions desperately invoke healing miracles behind you, you slide forward. You can still feel the lingering heat of Fusion Blast on your skin as you jump, lashing out toward the red blade with your own.

Your hands feel little resistance in response. The ash, all that's left of the nightwalkers, wafts up from under your feet as you slide forward again, trying to control your distance. Your opponent has pulled back, laughing at you all the while. You can see the grin through the rising steam.

This is bad.

"You have to get back...!" Female Bishop's voice comes at almost the same moment you bring up your sword. You heard it, you're almost sure: a mocking voice forming the words of a spell.

"*Ventus...lumen...libero!* Wind and light, release!"

You don't have time for a single passing thought. You don't sense pain or agony so much as simply emptiness. Sound disappears; the world around you vanishes. You don't know whether you are standing or sitting.

In reality, you've simply been knocked on your side. You open your mouth, but the groan that comes out along with your exhalation of breath means nothing to anyone. Only one thing is sure—the weight of your katana in your hand. You lean on it as you rise unsteadily to your feet, wavering like a ghost.

The presence— *There.*

Your companions lie fallen in this chamber. Female Warrior in a heap like a rag doll, Half-Elf Scout utterly motionless. Myrmidon Monk is slumped against one wall, your cousin kneeling beside him. Female Bishop lies prone on the ground—and then your eyes meet her sightless gaze.

"…I…an…till…fight…," she manages, her voice shaking, as she uses the sword and scales to stand, looking like she might collapse again at any moment. You feel the way she looks. Your chest armor hangs off you; you undo the ties and throw it away.

"A shame, a great shame. But I'm afraid your adventure ends here." The red blade is in front of you. The bastard is laughing. That armor won't do you any good now.

At last, you hold your sword straight and true before you, though it might be meaningless. The red blade is the symbol of death. You and your cousin, all your companions, are going to die.

There will be no exceptions. Not one.

For no one can escape the Death.

Very well.

Does it mean anything meeting your end with your sword at the ready?

"…!"

Someone is calling you in a voice like a scream. You hear the rattle of the gods' dice rolling.

And then, before you can answer, the red blade comes running, and blood sprays.

There's a girl of scant happiness.

Such is your first impression upon seeing her. The first thought you have upon opening the door of the famous Golden Knight, for she is the first thing you see.

Some adventurers fresh from the dungeon, their loot sitting before them, discuss the day's take:

"Eh, it's decent."

"C'mon, it's two hundred and fifty gold pieces. Not bad for a day's work, I'd say."

You can hear metal clinking against metal, some of it from coin, some from armor and weaponry. The footsteps of waiters and waitresses. The smell of food and wine. It all merges together into a wave of sensation that breaks upon you and then recedes, as if the dim tavern were an ocean unto itself.

The girl you spotted is in one corner, sitting with her shoulders hunched as if to make herself smaller. Even in the faint light and at this distance, you can see immediately that she has golden hair. She's small in stature. By her clothing, you would guess a cleric of some description. She looks to you like a woman who would drown in the tavern's sea of sound, sinking deeper and deeper until she disappeared completely.

You look at her, your vision obscured by your conical reed hat. She

©lack

seems out of place among the rough-and-tumble types who populate the tavern—but indeed she, too, is an adventurer.

Without really thinking about it, you press the blade at your hip farther into its scabbard, making sure it's still ready.

An adventurer.

That's what you came to this fortress city to become.

And now you are one.

There's a dwarf warrior, looking bored with a huge ax slung across his back. The lord of somewhere or other, complete with squire, is also lounging in shining armor. The one studying a scroll, struggling to memorize the words of a spell, must be an elf wizard. You even spot a rhea scout swipe some food off a table.

And on that same tabletop is a mountain of treasure the likes of which you've never seen.

So this is the fortress city.

"Hey, don't stare too hard. You want them to think you're a tourist?" a reproving voice says from somewhere just below your shoulder. "You've wanted to be an adventurer forever—don't screw it up by getting careless."

It's your cousin. She clutches the short wizard's staff she carries just in front of her bountiful chest. Despite her chiding tone, she's looking around with considerable interest herself.

Going off to hone your skills with a girl in tow—it's an embarrassment. That's how you feel anyway...

"Gosh, you'd never survive without your big sister around, would you?" she says, even though she's hardly older than you are, and even though you both left your home in the countryside for this city at the same time.

You sigh and shake your head. At least you have one companion you can count on. That's your half-elf scout, who's currently snickering to himself like you'd expect from a rhea. You jab his leather-covered shoulder with your elbow, and he responds, "Oops," his accent noticeable even in that single syllable. "Hey, Captain, don't get too worked up, eh? Just sit down and get a mug of ale—that's the first order of business."

"My, drinking at noon, are we?"

"Heh-heh! Listen, Sis, that's what adventurers do!"

Confronted by your cousin, you can only sigh. Are you sure at least one of them isn't a rhea?

"Well, elves and rheas are practically kin! Since I'm a half-elf, I guess that makes me a cousin."

"Oh, just like him and me!"

You consider pointing out that as long as she's keeping track, you're *second* cousins. Instead, you just sigh again.

Nonetheless, you agree with Half-Elf Scout. Your throat is parched. You've been walking around outside, and it's hot. You long for an ale. You nod at him, spot a convenient round table, and sit down on one of the barrels surrounding it. A waitress notices you immediately and comes rushing over, and you order three ales.

"Oh, if you have any water with fruit squeezed into it, I'll take that instead...," your cousin says.

You glance in your cousin's direction as you revise the order: two ales and a fruit water.

The waitress responds with a smile and bustles off to the kitchen. A doglike tail peeks out from under her skirt.

"Padfoot, huh?" Half-Elf Scout says. "Makes sense. The pay's good here."

Padfoots, with their occasional animallike features, often find it difficult to make a living wage in civilized society. Just a glance at her makes it clear how much money there is in this tavern and in this city.

All because of an underground labyrinth—the Dungeon of the Dead. Endless loot and riches bubbled up from it, along with endless monsters. The rumors—and the king's proclamation—were true, it seems. You nod again, adjusting the sword at your hip.

Shortly thereafter, the waitress reappears with three mugs, placing them on the table. You drink noisily. The ale is delicious.

"By the way," your cousin says, smiling brightly, "what's that girl doing?"

Argh.

Your cousin is pointing at the young woman you were looking at earlier.

"Hrm?" asks Half-Elf Scout, the one your cousin was consulting. He raises an eyebrow, then quickly says, "Ahhh. She's doing identification."

"Identification?"

"Stuff doesn't come out of that dungeon with a convenient little tag attached, right? You gotta ask somebody what it is. Otherwise no one'll buy it from you." Half-Elf Scout sips his drink.

When you ask if identification couldn't be done at a shop, he replies, "Yeah, but it'll cost ya. If a poor little wizard goes down in the dungeon all by their lonesome, they're almost guaranteed to die, even if they do everything right."

"And that's about the worst thing that could happen to you..."

"Sis, there's no end of bad things that could happen to you..."

You could turn into a zombie or monster food. Or worse fates that he hesitated to speak of.

You nod sagely as Half-Elf Scout trails off.

But if she can identify items, that means...

"So she serves the Supreme God, who sees the truth of all things," your cousin says. "And she's a bishop at that."

A bishop ranks at the top among clerics; it's a title one cannot claim without considerable intellectual prowess. It's always possible she's running a simple swindle, but she doesn't look like the type to you. Which would make her, you would think, in great demand...

"But if so, then she could have her pick of companions...," your cousin continues. You suggest that perhaps she's waiting for someone, but your cousin doesn't listen. You sigh.

As much as you're loathe to admit it in front of your cousin, spell casters possess crucial abilities. You know a few supernatural tricks of your own, but a warrior is no wizard. That girl at the table is in a position to pick and choose whom she adventures with—or at least, she should be.

"Good point," Half-Elf Scout says with a nod. "Gotta make sure it's someone you can trust."

He's right, you think. *Adventurer* has such a heroic ring, but in reality, many of them are broke, mendicant good-for-nothings. Especially now, with the dungeon to contend with, you hear that the standards of adventuring organizations have slipped. After all, even some of the most malnourished fighters can go down in the depths and, as you can see, come up with enough to fill their bellies and then some. All you need is a modicum of skill. That's adventurers today.

You like to think you are different from run of the mill troublemakers, but objectively speaking, there's little to distinguish you. You'll just have to let your actions do the talking…

"So let's take stock. I'm a scout, but I can handle the front row when I need to. Cap's a warrior, and, Sis, you're a spell caster…" Half-Elf Scout looks critically into his mostly empty mug as he speaks. "Usually, parties are four to six people—maybe another couple of casters would be nice."

"Wow, you really know your stuff!" your cousin says, her eyes sparkling. "Wait… Have you been down in the dungeon before…?!"

"Wh-who, me? Nah, nah, this is just, y'know, stuff I've heard from people… Ha, ha-ha." The scout chuckles half-heartedly and looks away. This is something about your cousin that you have unalloyed respect for.

"I've got an idea," she says, clapping her hands. "If she doesn't have a party and we need a spell caster, how about we ask that girl to join us?"

This is something about your *second* cousin that you are *trying* to have unalloyed respect for.

You're just starting to think seriously about the idea when:

"Yo, identifier!"

"You finish that stuff we asked you about yesterday?"

The voices are so loud that they cut through the hubbub of the tavern.

"?" Your cousin looks surprised. When you follow her gaze, you see why. Two adventurers who look to be of poor quality—right down to the state of disrepair of their equipment—have cornered the girl. Warriors, you suppose. Or perhaps scouts. They seem to lie vaguely somewhere in between.

The young woman flinches, then turns her head as if seeking the source of the voices. Finally, she replies stiffly, "Yes, sir. The items from yesterday are right here." From a bag beside her, she places several pieces of gear on the table, no less battered than the equipment the men are wearing themselves.

"Pig-Iron Sword? Rusty Chain Mail? Rotten Leather Armor?!" one of the men demands, his eyes getting wider with each item. "Hey, identifier, are you makin' fun of us?"

"I assure you, sir, I'm not! I would never...!" The woman denies it with pitiful vehemence, clutching her chest. In another time and another place, to question a bishop of the Supreme God in this manner could result in punishment for sheer impertinence.

"Sure hope you ain't. You know what'll happen to you if we find out you've been playing us, right?"

"Yeah, so make sure you identify our stuff right. Got it?"

"Yes, sir... Of course..." Then the girl silently turns and begins to work on the fresh pile of loot the men toss on the tabletop. She has a beautiful, almost dignified aspect, but her every movement seems hesitant, unsure. That by itself appears to annoy the men, for they audibly click their tongues several times. With each sound, the woman tenses, but she reaches assiduously for the gear, brushing her fingers over it.

"...They're a nasty bunch, huh?" your cousin whispers from behind her hand.

The tavern had gone quiet but only for an instant. The buzz soon returns, and the young woman's voice is lost in the chatter.

All this is perfectly normal, you figure. After a moment's thought, you call out to a waitress with long, rabbitlike ears who's passing by, pressing a small coin into her hand.

"Hoh," Half-Elf Scout says, raising an eyebrow in your direction. You ask the waitress about the young woman.

"Oh, her...," the harefolk waitress says. She tucks the coin into her ample bosom, takes a look around, and then continues in a conspiratorial tone. "She's an especially sad story. On her very first adventure, well, she got things a little bit wrong. That led her to come to the fortress city, but rumors of her failure spread."

"Common enough," Half-Elf Scout murmurs.

Your cousin's lips are pursed as if she can't quite accept the whole thing. "If at first you don't succeed, just try again, right?" she says.

"Adventurers are a superstitious lot. Luck's the coin of the realm, see," Half-Elf Scout replies.

"And so her companions left her behind," the harefolk waitress continues. "Now she makes her living identifying items..."

"Can't go adventuring all by herself. Bet she's lucky to make enough to eat, in fact. Rough times." *It's hard out here.*

You nod, then look once more in the girl's direction. Her voice still just barely carries over the chatter in the tavern.

"I'm sorry... I don't know what they are."

"Well, keep workin' on it till you *do* know. Damn worthless..."

"Yes, sir... I'm sorry, sir..."

"Betcha this is why she screwed up so badly, eh?"

"Yeah, you're right. It was a goblin hunt, wasn't it? Talk about worthless..."

"Yeah, in more ways than one!"

The men's lecherous cackling mocks the young woman. She curls into herself like a mouse.

You murmur something about their truly vile attitudes, but the waitress cocks her head and remarks that this is rather strange. "Those two are always a little rough, but they're not usually so aggressive."

"Hey," says your cousin, who's been listening silently, tugging on your sleeve. "The girl... How about we bring her on board?"

This is something about your cousin that you have unalloyed respect for.

"Hoh, Captain. Gonna make a move?"

You nod at Half-Elf Scout, then slowly stand up from your seat. You ask him to keep an eye on your cousin for a few minutes, to which he smiles and offers you these words of encouragement: "Put on a good show, Cap."

As you walk across the tavern, the eyes of the other adventurers settle upon you. You brush past waitresses and dodge legs stuck out to trip you up as a prank, never letting your smooth stride go interrupted.

The first one to notice your approach is the young woman, the one otherwise concentrating on her identifications. "E-excuse me, sir, but I'm currently busy with other customers. Perhaps you could wait a few minutes...?" Those words spill from lips that hardly form anything but a perfectly straight line: If her voice wasn't so faint, it would definitely sound like the ringing of a bell. Now that you're closer, you can see how petite the young woman is, her hands clasped uneasily in front of her modest chest.

Then your eyes open in surprise. Her eyes, set in that slim, lovely face—something must have happened to them, for they are clouded by a white mist and ringed by terrible scars. Maybe this explains her uncertain movements: She can't rely on her vision.

You shake your head with deliberate slowness, indicating that this is not a request for identification, before you turn to the two adventurers.

"'Ey, who the hell are you?!"

"Get lost! You wanna end up at the temple with your face smashed in?!"

When you point out that the way they're acting is no way to treat a woman, you receive only shouts of anger in return. Perhaps these people hail from some other land and don't understand what you're saying. You smile faintly.

"What a couple of brutes! Get 'em, Cuz!!"

Ah, dear cousin, always ready to pour oil on a fire. All the same, you sink down, angling your weight forward slightly, grasping the scabbard of your katana and striking backward with the ornamental hilt.

"Grgh?!" cries the adventurer you've just jabbed in the solar plexus. He must have gotten behind you in the couple of seconds you were distracted by your cousin. Nice move. You're impressed.

"Why, you…!" The other adventurer reacts quickly. In a single fluid motion, you rise up again, grip the scabbard with your left hand, and thrust it forward. "Hrgh?!" Another jab, another solar plexus. But your opponent is a big guy. That's not enough to bring him down.

And now he knows you're an enemy.

The two men jump back, looking at you with bloodshot eyes, and you return your hand to the sword at your hip, reassuming a ready posture. You keep the young woman, who looks as surprised as anyone, at your back, your feet sliding in half circles along the floor as you get ready for whatever's next.

"This bastard's a warrior…!"

"Nah, look! Not a scratch on that armor. He's more baby than warrior! Let's show him the ropes…!"

Can you do it?

A bead of sweat runs along your cheek. You drop deeper into your stance, making sure you have a firm grasp on the hilt of your sword. To draw your blade is to kill; this is the way of things. If you fail to kill, or to die, once your blade is set free, you will never escape dishonor.

For your cousin, you have no concern. If things go south, Half-Elf Scout will help her somehow. But you might die. And the trouble you cause might become trouble for the young woman before you. Those are the only two things that weigh on you. Only now do you begin to realize what a profound responsibility you've taken on without even thinking. You're facing warriors who have been down in the dungeon. Two of them, at that. You don't know what they're capable of.

Your opponents are wearing body armor. You don't think you'll be able to stop them just by lopping off an arm or a leg.

You do have some confidence in your technique. Your objective will be to score a critical hit with your opening stroke, decapitating the first adventurer, then killing the second on the return. If you don't manage it, they'll drag you down and gut you like a freshly caught fish.

You take a deep breath in and let a shallow one out. You feel around with your feet, clad in animal-skin socks and split-toed sandals, searching for footing. You grasp the scabbard firmly with your left hand, your right gripping the hilt. You can't let sweat cause your hands to slip.

Draw? Don't draw? You will draw. You will. Draw. Draw. Cut. Now—!

"Will you keep it down over here, you louts?!"

With that one shout, the hum of the tavern crowd comes back like a ringing in your ears. The explosive atmosphere dissipates, replaced by the collective murmurs of the patrons. You look over to discover that someone belonging to a party camped out at the backmost table in the building has gotten to his feet.

"Hmph." He looks like a young lion to you with sharp, handsome features. His movements are elegant, aristocratic. The cast of his face is composed but slim; at first glance, he doesn't look like someone who belongs in a tavern full of people looking to delve the Dungeon of the Dead. But behold: The man is wearing shining armor. It glints in the unsteady tavern light, clearly made of diamond.

More surprising still, it appears well used. Though it shines, it shows signs of wear, unlike your own chest guard; it completely changes your first impression of the man. You see now that he must be a knight of some renown.

"I-it ain't like that, Lord," stutters one of the men who had been menacing the young woman. "We was just teachin' a newbie what's what when he tried to butt in on our conversation…"

"Y-yeah, that's right. We weren't tryin' to bother you or anything…"

The diamond knight doesn't respond immediately, though. He looks at you, then at the pile of gear on the tabletop, then at the young woman, her face drawn in fear. Finally, his gaze returns to the adventurers, and he says softly, "I see all your items have been identified." It's not a question. The men nod. "Then you have no more business with this young woman. Sit quietly and have a drink or get out of here."

The two adventurers look about to say something, but the knight's menacing aura overwhelms them, and in the end, they stay quiet. Finally, with frustrated clicks of their tongues, they shove the gear off the table and back into their bag. "Very good," the knight says, like a master acknowledging the work of his servants. The men slink away, their steps sullen, the young woman vacantly watching them go with her sightless eyes.

You have, it would appear, been rescued. You express your thanks, but the knight shakes his head. "I admire your passion, but not your methods. The gulf in strength between those who have braved the dungeon and those who haven't is simply too great."

You yourself have no choice but to acknowledge this. You had hoped to resolve things peacefully but quickly found yourself in over your head and had nearly had to draw your sword. Those men knew how to handle themselves. You aren't confident things would have ended well for you if you really had drawn. Your inexperience is what got you into that mess. You thought you could control the situation. But this only makes you realize how far you are from being able to dictate the course of events.

The knight says "Don't worry about it" and smiles, recognizing that your actions were honorable. "But don't let your guard down, either," he adds. "Those men were a party of six yesterday." You cock your head at this, and the diamond knight continues as if it was of scant consequence. "Tonight, they're two. The other four lost their souls."

Consumed by the Death in the dungeon.

Someone snickers softly. Amid the burble of the tavern, the sound is like a bubble rising on a river and bursting. You understand now. Perhaps the men had meant to go back home. That was why they were so scared, so overawed. They didn't want to admit that their spirits had been broken.

"Take care, good sir," the knight says, slapping you on the shoulder, and then his eyes open a little wider, and he smiles. "That's a fine saber you have there."

At the far table, the diamond knight's friends say something mocking about his actions. He shoots something back, then turns slowly on his heel and returns to his place. At long last, you let out a breath you didn't realize you'd been holding in and relax your grip on your sword.

What a scene!

You discover your palms are slick with sweat, and your heart is racing from nervousness and excitement.

And you haven't even been down in the dungeon yet.

"Gosh, here we were gonna come and help, but I guess you didn't need us." Surprised by the voice behind you, you let out a great sigh. Apparently, you didn't even notice Half-Elf Scout and your cousin coming up to you.

"That was a knight's knight, huh? It would sure be encouraging to have someone like him around," your cousin says.

"Eh, kinda feel like he stole our boy's thunder, though. So?" Half-Elf Scout asks, and you nod.

"Ah, ahem...er...," the young woman stammers in bewilderment.

The first thing that's needed is a proper conversation with this girl.

§

You are an adventurer.

You heard the rumors about the infamous Dungeon of the Dead and came to the fortress city in hopes of delving to its lowest level. That's all there is to your story thus far, so you recite your simple explanation with assurance.

Your cousin, after your rather brief tale, turns a smile on the young woman across from you and says, "See?" Almost a whisper. "He'd lose his own head if it wasn't stuck on his neck. I had to come with him because I was afraid he'd never make it on his own."

Well, who cares what your *second* cousin thinks? You shake your head gently. Much as you hate to admit it, she has learned a lot about magic—but who goes on an adventure in heels?

You ignore your *second* cousin—puffing out her cheeks and insisting that her shoes are perfectly cute—and turn to your scout.

"Ah. Me, I plan t'smoke out every secret in that dungeon and make my name known across the Four-Cornered World," Half-Elf Scout says, a motivation more redolent of human than elf ancestry. He smacks himself on his chest, which he puffs out proudly. "That's why the cap's passion for testing himself against the dungeon connected with me, and I decided to go along with him."

"I know it must've been rough for you," your cousin says with a grin, "stuck up in that tree after that wizard you pranked cast a bug-attraction spell on you."

"A-*hem*," Half-Elf Scout says, mustering a dry laugh, and the young woman across from you visibly relaxes, albeit only a little.

"For me…" Her voice when she opens her mouth sounds so fragile. "I, too, once intended as much."

"Intended what?"

"The dungeon… To do—*something* about it."

History shows that peace inevitably ends; since the Age of the Gods, this has ever been the way of the Four-Cornered World. The shadows of the Dark Gods move behind the scenes; illness spreads. The world grows ever more disordered, and people's hearts become ever more a wilderness. And then—the Death. Yes, that is the true problem.

Those who succumb to the plague arise once more in unlife to attack the living. Those living become one of the dead, and they, too, rise to consume other people, and the dead increase in number once more: Catastrophe grows and spreads.

If these were simply undead, perhaps a great muster of monks or clerics could have defended against them somehow. But it was found that prayer for the repose of their souls had no effect. It was not so simple. These were no mere wandering spirits.

The whirlwind of Chaos continued to spread. The forces of Order were swallowed up, and it seemed only a matter of time before all returned to darkness.

Find the source of this Death and destroy it: the king's admonition— was it too late or just in time? It was not long after that some adventurers did in fact discover the Dungeon of the Dead.

It is said monsters emerge endlessly from the dungeon depths.

It is said in the dungeon there, likewise, await endless riches.

It is said in the dungeon's deepest reaches resides a Demon Lord.

The king of the land immediately dispatched an army, but every man was swallowed by the labyrinth, and none came home. The military was never made to brave the traps and fearsome dangers of the dungeon. Their purpose is to stand ready to repel the savages from the north who range across the mountains, the barbarians from the southern reaches, and every neighboring country that constantly looks for an opportune moment to strike. They might even meet a great army of Chaos in the field—but dungeons? Those are for adventurers.

And thus the fortress city arose. A home base built hard on the mouth of the dungeon to serve those adventurers who ventured within. Adventurers who sought fame, fortune, and the head of the Demon Lord...

"Kill a few monsters, and you can earn more in a day than you'd see in a lifetime in your backwater village!"

"True, but you never know when you're going to die down there."

"Then what say we forget about the Demon Lord and just make our money farming those monsters?"

There is no sign as yet that the Dungeon of the Dead will be destroyed anytime soon.

You lay all this out, and the young woman replies "That's right" softly and nods. "And I thought, rather than spend my life shut away in the temple...I wanted to at least try to do something to better this world..."

So she had come to the fortress city in the hope of finding companions and delving the dungeon. A splendid resolve. You tell her so earnestly. It's not something that's so simple to do. As a matter of fact, you yourself have not come here with any lofty ambitions of saving the world, so you are not one to judge. It is up to each person to decide how they will live and how they will die. It is not your place to debate the merits of their choices.

To still be able to act with others in mind when all that is the case—that is truly admirable.

But now you have a question. Surely, she need not sit here, identifying items, when she could be down in the dungeon.

The young woman tenses when you mention this, her breathing shallow. "I'm very sorry," she says. She pours water from a canteen into her mug, some of it spilling onto the table, and then drinks. "I… I…" Then she takes several long, deep breaths and finally manages to get out the words. "I once—before I came to the fortress city, before I entered the temple—went on an adventure."

You're about to ask what that has to do with anything when a sharp pain runs through your side. Your cousin, never letting her smile slip, has jabbed you with her elbow. "Let me guess," she says, trying to help the hesitant young woman. "Your companions…?"

Yes. The young woman nods, her slim shoulders trembling as she looks at the table. "They said someone who was once defeated by goblins… That the dungeon would be too dangerous for the likes of her… And so they left me behind." She smiles, albeit fleetingly.

Goblins. Everyone knows they are some of the weakest creatures in the Four-Cornered World, hardly worth bothering with. They attack villages, destroy crop fields, abduct women, rape, and gorge themselves, and they are no smarter than nasty children.

No big deal.

In the Dungeon of the Dead, there is an endless array of creatures far more threatening than goblins. If you have a sword in your hand and a wish to save the world in your heart, goblins hardly merit a thought.

Of course, just moments ago, you were questioning whether you could even deal with two adventurers who had been down in the depths…

"On that…first adventure," the young woman says, "I made…a mistake. That's why I retired to the temple…"

Before you can say anything, your cousin has poked you in the ribs again. You glance at her with a *That hurt*, but your *second* cousin all but ignores you. You clear your throat and begin to open your mouth again. What need is there for her to stay here and be treated like a common item wrangler or to tell her story to anyone else? You know it sounds harsh to say, but surely she has no reason to remain here in the fortress city, this place of bitter memories.

"Well, I…" For a moment, she trails off, embarrassed. But then she squeezes out the words: "I want to bring peace to the world. Even if I can't adventure myself, I thought if I could do anything at all to contribute to the end of that dungeon…"

So anything that might help save the world, you think.

The young woman looks at the ground and goes silent. She lets out only the occasional soft groan, her shoulders shaking. You say nothing about it but take a quick glance at your companions.

"Er, ah, r-right. I think it's…just fine," your cousin says, shooting a hesitant look at Half-Elf Scout.

"Good by me," he says with a wave of his hand. "Heck, kinda feel like I'd curse myself if I complained. So why not?"

You nod at them, then inform the young woman that you're searching for a bishop to join the party.

"What…?" she says, glancing up in surprise at that title.

You tell her that according to what you've heard, bishops are the only clerics granted the ability to identify items. To be a bishop, one would inevitably have mastered at least some magic, so to have one around would be heartening.

"Ah—ahem, there's no need to fuss over me. I'm used to being laughed at…" She smiles weakly, almost sulking, and then her lightless eyes drift toward you. "If… If you would like to have an item identified, there's no need for all this show. I'm more than willing to help you."

From the way she behaves, you can imagine how this young woman has been treated. You shake your head—*You misunderstand*—and ask if she doesn't know any bishops.

"I wish I could help you, but I'm afraid not. There are no bishops among my clientele…"

'No, no.' You shake your head once more. *'Is there not a bishop before our eyes?'*

This provokes a look of surprise from the young woman, and she stares at you. Her features, you note, are statuesque. Or would be without the wounds around her eyes— No, in fact, even so. Perhaps more so.

"But—but I've never even been into the dungeon yet... And I was defeated by goblins...!"

"Y'ain't the only one who's never set foot in the dungeon," Half-Elf Scout reassures the terrified young woman. "But so what?" He laughs. "Neither has the captain or Sis here. Like little birds just leaving the nest, all of us."

"He's right," your cousin says, calmly taking up the theme with a smile. "I'm an untested wizard, and my little brother—" *Your cousin.* "You can see he's all talk so far... *Sigh!*" Your *second* cousin lets out a dramatic sigh but makes it look natural. "If we had a cleric around to put him in his place every once in a while, I'd sure feel better about things!"

....

You refuse to unreservedly agree with your *second* cousin, but it's true that you need a healer. You limit yourself to giving your *second* cousin a good glare, then clear your throat before finally speaking again. You tell the young woman that if she's willing, you would be happy to have her as a member of your team.

"—...!"

The young woman is flummoxed for a second by your suggestion, but then her lips draw into a line, and she reaches out uncertainly. You offer your own rough hands in response, feeling her slim fingers touch your palms. Their grip is weak, and they tremble slightly, but...

"If you'll have me, then gladly," she says, and for the first time, she gives you a heartfelt smile. You answer by clasping her hands firmly.

§

"So how about we have a little look-see at the temple?" suggests Half-Elf Scout when he judges that Female Bishop has begun to calm down. "Might be able to pick something up. Divine guidance, y'know?"

You don't particularly have any better ideas, so you nod your agreement. You each take some coins out of your purses and pay, then leave the tavern behind.

"If we're going to form a party, it's going to be everyone's money."
Your cousin, walking along in her high heels (!), has the frustrating
habit of occasionally saying something insightful. True, the cost of
gear—weapons and armor, items, and other things that will contribute
to everyone's collective chances of survival—will be a shared concern.
With an eye on the future, you should probably pool your resources,
and the first thing you'll do is buy your cousin a new pair of shoes.

"Aw, but they're cute. It's fine. And the dungeon has a stone floor,
right?"

Curse this *second* cousin of yours. It's impossible to argue when you're
not sure if she's joking.

You keep discovering more things you don't know about this town
and about the dungeon. Then again, you just got here. Maybe it's not
something to lose any sleep over.

"...I've been to the temple here once, to pay my respects," Female
Bishop says softly, interrupting your thoughts. "I remember it as a
place overflowing with adventurers, so perhaps we'll find someone..."

From the fact that the staff she holds depicts the symbol of the sword
and scales, you know she worships the Supreme God. But which deity
does this fortress city's temple primarily worship?

"The Trade God," Female Bishop adds pointedly. She almost
sounds excited; maybe she's pleased to be able to help. "The patron
deity of wind, commerce, and travel. Ahem..." This second part of
her speech is rather quieter, as though she suddenly realized how she
might be coming across and grew embarrassed.

"Well, that sounds profitable!" Half-Elf Scout replies. "After
all, travel and commerce mean meetings and money!" You look
around, trying to decide which way to go. Every city and fortress has
something—a shrine, a temple, or in smaller places, a chapel. The
object of worship may vary from place to place, but there's always at
least one. It seems a refuge for prayer is needed wherever people go to
battle. Even if you personally don't completely understand it.

Your feelings as an individual, though, are not the issue; from a
practical perspective, you fully comprehend the need for healers. It
was your own good fortune that you met Female Bishop—the young
woman who now trots along at the very rear of your formation. But

spell slingers are few and far between. They are some of the only ones who can manifest their talent and intelligence directly into the world—in the form of magic.

"Look at all these shops. I thought it was just adventurers around here!" your *second* cousin marvels, gawking in amazement. Looking at her, you personally wouldn't assume intelligence was a wizard's primary trait...

Much as it pains you to admit it, though, she's right. Most of the people milling around on the fortress city's great main thoroughfare are bedecked in weapons and armor—they're adventurers—but many aren't. These other people, you suppose, must have been drawn to the city in the hopes of relieving the adventurers of some of the many riches they'd gathered out of the depths.

The streets of the fortress city are haphazard and hard to navigate; at first, you found it difficult even to go in a straight line. After five minutes of walking, it's all too obvious that the city is a labyrinth unto itself.

It's no surprise that the Trade God should have a temple here. After all, in the depths of the Dungeon of the Dead lies loot aplenty. Looking down the street, you see the obvious sorts of places: inns and taverns, armorers' shops—but also places selling fancy clothes, restaurants, even the occasional gambling den. Yes, this makes sense. Without some way to spend your earnings, gemstones are just rocks, and gold coins are simply pretty bits of metal.

"C'mon—aren't you embarrassed, gawking so openly like that?" your cousin says, elbowing you again when she catches you taking a particularly long look at what you suspect is a house where you might find female company. In her hand is an item you don't recognize: a piece of cloth for tying hair back.

You question when she got it, to which she replies, "Just now," and sticks out her bountiful chest proudly. "Geez, I know guys can be oblivious, but you're worse than most. Here, come on."

"Er? Oh..." Female Bishop looks confused after your cousin called out to her. "Me...?"

"Yes, you. Turn around, if you please." Then your *second* cousin spins Female Bishop around and holds up the cloth. You think she's about to tie back Female Bishop's hair, but instead the cloth goes around her sightless eyes. "There, how do you like that? I tried to pick something that would feel nice." Then your cousin takes Female Bishop's hand and turns her back around. The vicious burns that robbed her of her sight are neatly covered by the bandage.

"I know I must have been...rather unpleasant to look at..." Female Bishop's voice trembles with what seems like trepidation.

But your cousin sounds honestly puzzled as she shakes her head and replies, "Not at all. This way just makes you look mysterious—and pretty, to boot!"

Right? She smiles in your direction, looking for confirmation. From an expression of confusion, Female Bishop's face scrunches up. Your cousin quickly puts a hand on her back. "S-sorry, was it wrong of me? If you don't like black, we could get, uh, a white cloth, or blue, or... how about pink?!"

Female Bishop shakes her head, sending ripples through her golden hair. Half-Elf Scout grins. You let out a breath and smile. This is something about your cousin that you have unalloyed respect for, but...

Curse this *second* cousin of yours. You look well down the thoroughfare in an attempt to hide your smile.

That's when it happens. A gust of wind blows down the street, carrying the stagnant air off into the sky. You close your eyes against the bracing wind, then follow it with your gaze as it rushes away into the heavens. That's when you spot a spire towering beyond the nearby rooftops. They probably thought anyone would look up when the wind blew. For atop the tower stands a windmill, cranking noisily in the gusts of air.

Yes indeed. You nod once again.

This town did need a temple to the Trade God.

§

"Apostates, and stingy to boot—get out of here!"

You're greeted by the words of a nun, her willowy impression (complete with modest endowment) is completely blown away by the force of her pronouncement as she flings open the doors.

"Dammit! Apostates, my ass, you greedy priests…!"

Perhaps the temple refused to lift a curse placed upon them in the dungeon, or to heal their wounds, or maybe the disagreement was over a Resurrection miracle. Whatever the case, an adventurer in full armor rushes out of the temple past you, carrying a companion.

Vast windows let in the light and diffuse it through a stone chapel, bathing everything up to the altar in somber illumination. This hardly looks like a place to be speaking of money. So when your cousin mutters, "I'm not sure what to say…," you think you understand what she means.

Then again, you haven't come to ask for healing. Whether your purse is light or your wallet thin, you have nothing to fear.

But the fortress city truly is a town of adventurers!

You look around, seeing men and women in all kinds of gear praying. Perhaps they seek success in battle, or a safe return home, or a successful recovery for wounded comrades. At this temple, it's said that not only are there healers but even clerics of high-enough rank to perform the Resurrection miracle. To invoke this miracle, to bring someone back from the edge of death, the cleric must calm their own soul and pray fervently. To repeat, spell casters are all too rare already. Let alone highly ranked ones. And then there's the fact that certain ceremonies that would fail if performed in the dungeon might be a different story when carried out in the temple precincts with incense burning. You've heard how many an adventurer has collected piles of money and come to this temple with a request…

"Please don't get the wrong impression." It seems the nun has noticed you're new here. She nods to you in welcome, and there's a smile like a flower on her lovely face. She waves the indulgence slip she's holding, twisting her narrow hips. The movement makes clear that the line of her body is as straight as carved stone. "Anyone who *doesn't* make the mistake of thinking they need make no offering when they request a miracle is warmly welcomed here.

"Although if you lack faith, there might not be a miracle anyway."

Half-Elf Scout looks a bit stricken at this whispered addendum.

"Hmm?" the nun says, noticing his chagrin without ever letting her smile slip. "Something the matter?"

"Huh? Nah, just, we're new in town. Thought we might say hello, introduce ourselves in case we needed any help later…"

"I see! What a lovely idea!"

"So, uh, lookin' forward to your help if we show up on the edge of death…" The scout looks increasingly uncomfortable in the face of the eager nun.

This was, after all, the front line of the war against the Death. It wasn't only the pious faithful who showed up to pray. Many present were adventurers, castoffs from who knew where, seeking a miracle. If the temple simply granted all requests at no charge out of the goodness of their hearts, they would soon find themselves being ripped off and exploited in every which way.

The gods were merciful, but they were also just. Receiving a boon from their followers was permitted only after repentance.

I think I get it now: No one believes in the gods so fervently as someone hanging from a cliffside.

"Ah—ahem—th-this isn't much, but…" Female Bishop reaches a slim arm between the two of you (she can't have guessed what you're thinking, can she?) and hands the nun a few small coins. The other woman takes them, counts them carefully, then wraps them in a cloth for holding donations.

We'll definitely need to establish a common purse for the party.

"Thank you kindly," the nun says, her manner softening—and then she sees Female Bishop's face and blinks. "Say, aren't you…?" You think perhaps she's about to remark on the scars that even serving the gods can't seem to remedy, but instead she says, "I see. Found yourself some companions, have you? Perhaps that, too, is the gods' guidance." And the nun traces a holy sigil in front of herself in lovely, flowing motions.

Now you see. She is a cleric after all.

While you're having this somewhat inappropriate thought, your cousin butts in: "That's rude." You ignore her and look at Half-Elf Scout. Whatever he was hoping to "pick up"—is it here?

"Good point," he says. "Say, Sister. Mind if we pick out an adventurer?"

"Feel free," the nun replies with a smile. "Our lord is the master of meetings and partings as well, after all." Then she bows her head with an elegant motion and bids them a good day before disappearing deeper into the temple.

You ask what's going on. "I've only heard rumors," Half-Elf Scout begins. But then he says, "There's supposed to be this miracle Preservation."

This temple, it seems, doesn't simply abandon the wounded to die. Of course, there are many who are simply beyond help, no matter how many prayers are said over their shattered bodies, but for an appropriate donation, the people of this temple are more than happy to say a benediction. And just because a person at death's door has no money doesn't mean the priests are so heartless as to leave them to their fate. Those wounded who have breath, however faint, left in their bodies but who cannot afford an appropriate offering are put to sleep with a miracle until that day when their companions can bring the money they need.

"It don't last forever is what I hear, but still. Not to mention, Preservation is like Resurrection—needs *faith*." On this last word, Half-Elf Scout curls his fingers in a gesture that clearly means *money* and then gives a helpless shrug. "And let's just say a lotta people go down in the dungeon in hopes of becoming a lot more faithful."

Ah. Now you understand. If a party has been so thoroughly battered that it has reached this stage of desperation, then almost by definition, it lacks the strength to challenge the dungeon. Half-Elf Scout intends to find some such adventurer and try to get them to join your party, even temporarily.

"Sounds like a lot of 'em just get left behind… Or so they say," he adds, staring down the hallway the nun disappeared into—but looking a bit unsettled. Some might come close to earning the money they need only to be destroyed again; others could find new party members or simply leave town altogether…

There were also adventurers now awaiting companions who would never return. How many such forgotten men and women slept here in this temple? Who knows? You yourself might be one someday.

"So my thinking is, we have one of 'em, any one of 'em, brought back. Consider the healing fee a debt." Half-Elf Scout speaks lightly, as if to dispel your concerns. "After all, not like we can pay it out of pocket!"

"I would prefer to avoid such methods if possible…," Female Bishop says, her face drawn. Maybe she's thinking along the same lines as you are. You voice your agreement. In any event, it's a last resort. Not a choice that will be open to you until you have some money.

Your discussion is interrupted by the approach of a heavy sound. *Scrape, scrape, scrape, scrape, scrape.* Whatever they are, there are five of them: hempen bags, soaked with some dark-red substance. Each one, tied with a rope, is just about big enough for a person to fit inside.

"What's going on…?" your cousin says, cocking her head, perplexed. You mutter that those are body bags. And by the looks of it, the person dragging them along is an adventurer.

"Any priests around here? I'd like to request five burials." It's the very definition of an enchanting voice. There stands a gorgeous woman, all elegant curves and ample bosom, clad in black. In her hand is a spear, and the bloody bandages wrapped here and there around her body suggest she's a warrior just back from the dungeon.

"Burials?" replies a priest in a businesslike tone. "Have you informed the next of kin?"

"Not sure it matters. I don't think they know anyone else here—I sure don't." The warrior's tone is matter-of-fact, her words mercifully ruthless.

"Then I'll start the procedures for burial," the priest says with a bow, and the woman puts down the pack she's carrying. It's better than a body bag but still heavy, and as it hits the stone floor of the temple, it jangles loudly.

Equipment. You understand intuitively. It's the gear that belonged to the dead adventurers. It's perfectly clear now that this woman is an adventurer whose party was completely wiped out, aside from her. She brushes her cheek with an exhausted motion, letting out a sigh as she brushes her hair lazily back over her shoulders.

"Oh…," Female Bishop murmurs quietly. She's been listening very closely, and now her sightless eyes settle on the female warrior.

Remembering what happened earlier, you stay vigilant, hand on the hilt of your sword, as you say, *'You know her?'*

"Yes," Female Bishop answers with a nod. "Ahem, she's an adventurer…" Female Bishop stops there, looking deeply discouraged to realize she doesn't need to explain this. Maybe she isn't very used to conversation. You shake your head and tell her not to worry, encourage her to continue. "She's been kind enough to speak to me before, at the tavern," Female Bishop explains. "At least, I think that's her." Considering the state of her vision, it must be hard to tell. You're nodding your acknowledgment when:

"Good heavens, I can at least introduce my own self."

The voice comes from beside you, unexpectedly, and you take a quick step back.

She got the drop on you.

The woman smiles at you from just steps away. You can smell a sweet fragrance on her hair mixed with the scents of blood and dust.

She takes a sliding step forward, into striking distance of you. She's about your own age, and though you thought you were watching her, you never saw her start to move.

Is this what it means to be a veteran of the dungeon?

You mentally chide yourself for your lapse—maybe she notices, maybe she doesn't, but either way, she brings her hands together in front of her large chest. "Hee-hee—finally found yourself some friends, eh? That's good. I was starting to worry about you."

"Er, oh, yes," replies Female Bishop with a fretful nod. "Only just now…"

"Well, nice to meet you, O brave leader," Female Warrior says, casting her eyes slowly in your direction. Then she utters a number you don't quite follow. "I'm a freelance fighter. Fresh back on the market…" She flashes you a sweetheart smile; you nod hesitantly and introduce yourself in return. When you tell her you just came to the fortress city and are looking for companions, she says, "That so?" The look in her eye is practiced; you would hardly imagine she had just requested burial for five of her party members. But what was that number she gave you…?

"Oh, that's my identification number. Might as well be my name. I became an adventurer instead of paying taxes, so—you see? No big deal." You notice your cousin shifting uncomfortably behind you. You don't particularly agree with the warrior's choice, but since she herself doesn't seem to mind it, you have no reason to argue.

Your cousin, it would seem, feels differently. "Um... Are you okay?" She sounds uneasy but nonetheless addresses Female Warrior directly.

"Oh, perfectly," the fighter responds with a disinterested wave of her hand. "I only just met them in the tavern yesterday anyway. It's tougher the first time."

That little addition causes your cousin to choke out, "The dungeon... You went down there, didn't you?" She gulps audibly.

"Well, I only made it as far as the first room before I came running home." Female Warrior—you hesitate to think of her by the number she gave you—looks at you again. A pointed, almost flirtatious glance that would certainly invite a misunderstanding from many a man she turned it on... "I'd be very happy if you'd invite me along. I may not look like much, but I'm better than your big sister there."

Considering the offer, you never take your hand off your weapon nor your eyes off the other warrior as you ask everyone, "What do you think?"

"Another beautiful woman? No complaints from me," Half-Elf Scout pipes up.

"Ha-ha!" Female Warrior laughs, then whispers, "I'm flattered." Is it just your imagination, or do you hear a hint of a threat underneath the remark?

"Me, I guess...I'm perfectly happy to have more women in the group," your cousin says. "And if she's already been in the dungeon, so much the better."

Female Bishop doesn't say anything—perhaps she doesn't think you were asking her. She's been listening silently, but at your urging, she says quickly, "Oh, yes." Nothing more than that, and you decide to take it as agreement.

So that's everyone. And yet...

"Heh-heh. What? Something the matter?" Female Warrior asks before you can open your mouth.

She's sharp.

She may be even more perceptive than you, despite all the training you've done learning to read people and situations. After intense consideration, you tell her that you wish to see what she can do in a single move. You have no objection to inviting her along, you say, but you want to know what she's capable of. This party is your responsibility, however temporary it may be. Insofar as ability corresponds directly to life and death, it behooves you to know how strong your party members are… No, you say finally, that's all an excuse. You have no choice but to admit that you were secretly excited just now. You're picturing those adventurers from before, old hands of the dungeon: You came this close to testing yourself against them but didn't get the chance. You won't hide your desire to know whether your skills can match hers.

"Hmm. Well, when you put it that way…"

You almost *feel* the look in her eyes change…

The quiet *thump* as she leaps in and the *hush* of your sword sliding out of its scabbard come almost simultaneously. You duck forward, rising up as you draw and strike from below. There's a rush of air, and the tip of your blade meets the haft of her spear with a *clang*. At that moment, the tip of her spear is already over your head—even though it was at throat height an instant ago. Though the tip of the spear is currently covered, a good chop with it would at least have knocked you out. You flick the spear away with the back of your blade, holding the grip with just one hand, then return your other hand to the hilt just in time to prepare to bring it down. By then, Female Warrior has adjusted her own grip on her weapon and is preparing to stab again…

"Ha!" Her laugh is as much exhalation as mirth, and you see the aggression in her eyes soften. "I'm only sorry we agreed on just one move. I would've liked to see how that played out." She spins the spear around before tapping the butt against the floor, and you nod slowly at her. The first move was evenly matched, if only just. The second? You're not sure how it would have gone.

"What do you think you're doing, whipping your sword at a woman you just met?! Your big sister is very angry!" Your big sister, sure—that would be your cousin. You make a face like you just swallowed something bitter. You know you've done your share of training. Nor did you discount her simply because she took the offer on the spot. But it turns out that even a little experience in the dungeon—if you come back alive—makes a world of difference.

"U-um, what…? What exactly are you two doing…?" Female Bishop asks uneasily, not having understood what was going on.

"Never you mind," Half-Elf Scout says. "They're not fighting. Or maybe they are, but you know what they say: The more you fight, the closer you get."

'Probably,' you respond, turning back to the others and bowing your head. What just happened was entirely a personal indulgence, all due to your own inexperience.

"Ugh, I can't believe you!" your cousin cries, but you think this is good. In fact...

"Not to put too fine a point on it," comes a chilly voice from behind you, "but those who are faithless enough to engage in violence right in the temple might very well deserve to be turned to ash, don't you think?" You turn around to see the nun from before, her face studiously expressionless.

You can't find anything to say, but from beside you, Female Warrior pipes up—"Yes'm"—with a pleasant smile.

"You understand I'm not joking, yes?"

"Of course, miss, certainly. Very sorry."

"For goodness' sake." The nun heaves a sigh at Female Warrior, who shows no sign of feeling particularly guilty. "Be that as it may... This *is* a place of meetings and partings. May a favorable wind blow before you. May it blow all the way to the deepest depths of the dungeon." The nun traces the holy sigil again.

You understand now that this town really does need this temple.

In any event, you know how you feel about Female Warrior: Now you wonder if you met *her* standards...

"Let's see...," she says to this, putting a hand to her cheek thoughtfully. "I've got no complaints—take it you don't, either?" And then she flashes you a sharklike smile.

§

There's a screech of metal, and a steel ball the size of your fist goes flying into the night sky. An elf picks up the Wizball, which carries a death curse, with his bare hands.

The crowd gathered in the arena on the edges of the fortress city raises a hearty cheer. You aren't very familiar with the rules of this game, but you gather that this move scored some points. The elves in the audience stamp their feet as the white numbers change on a black-board high above.

The stadium is utter cacophony. People shout, cheer, and taunt. Vendors work their way along the narrow aisles, likewise shouting, "Wine, bread, cat meat."

Even you almost feel overwhelmed—you can't imagine how Female Bishop must be feeling at this moment. She's pale, pressing a hand to her forehead, but when you ask if she's all right, she nods bravely. "I—I was just a little taken aback... I'm fine."

"Yeah, it's like some kind of festival!" your *second* cousin says, staring openly at the crowd.

You ask Half-Elf Scout what exactly is going on. "I guess when you spend all day risking your life, you like to relax by watching other people risk theirs," he says. It sounds so simple. You nod.

You do understand that it's easier to be amused by events that don't directly concern you. In the stadium below, a party led by a ranger is pitching the steel ball to a party led by a warlock. Even your cousin cringes as you hear flesh squish and see blood fly, but meanwhile...

"Hmm. Pretty sure he's usually around here," says Female Warrior. She's the one who brought you to this stadium.

§

Adventuring parties that dare to challenge the dungeon usually con-sist of six people at most. That's partly because of the restrictive width of the dungeon's corridors, but it also allows one to keep track of all members in a party and make sure nobody falls behind. If nothing else, the nation itself has already demonstrated that simply sending soldiers en masse is nothing more than a recipe for feeding the Death. Six people is also, it might be said, roughly the largest group in which everyone can all look after their own equipment and resources. It would be no laughing matter if someone was eaten by a monster while trying to balance the account books.

And so—six people.

From that perspective, you could do with finding one more party member. A warrior or a spell caster? Beggars can't be choosers, but someone who knows a bit of magic would be nice.

"I'm sure *you* can sling a spell or two, can't you?" Female Warrior says in response to this remark, smiling again. You're just leaving the temple. Maybe she figured it out when the two of you were squaring off. You nod the affirmative, and she nods back, satisfied. "And that girl there, she must know some magic."

This time she turns to the person walking at the very back of your line, Female Bishop.

"I do, too!" your *second* cousin interjects; you ignore her and question Female Bishop instead.

"Only minor spells, but yes. I know some of the ways of magic use."

That being the case, then out of the five of you, you have three spell casters: yourself, your cousin, and Female Bishop. You wonder if Half-Elf Scout might not have something up his sleeve as well. You glance at him, but he waves his hand dismissively. "Not me," he says.

What about this final person, then?

"How about a monk?" Female Warrior asks. "I know someone I could introduce you to…"

§

Female Warrior's introduction is exactly what you need.

Then again, you think as she leads you to the arena, *maybe it's a clever bit of work on her part*. Bring her friend into the party to help secure her own position. You're a bit taken aback by how naturally she managed it.

"Are there really monks in a place like this?" your cousin asks.

"Heh-heh— Sure there are. Don't know how serious they are about their spirituality, though," Female Warrior says, spotting the person she's looking for among the crowd. She tells you to wait for a moment, then slips away through the mass of people.

A moment later, she returns, trailed by a lithe figure who literally stands head and shoulders above the crowd. His face looks like that of an insect—this is the first time you've seen one of these strange beings up close, but you know he's a Myrmidon. A Myrmidon monk.

"Huh, so you're the ones looking for a monk?" the Myrmidon says almost disinterestedly, his mandibles clacking together. His antennae bob as he takes you in before producing a dramatic sigh. "Women and children and one *identifier*. Are you really adventurers?"

Female Bishop doesn't so much as flinch at these cold words. Perhaps you shouldn't be surprised, considering what she endured as recently as a few hours earlier, but your cousin looks at him scathingly. "Master Monk. I hardly think that's any way to talk to two women you've just met. True, we're inexperienced, but still…"

"I'm only saying what everyone around you sees when they look at you. You need to be aware of it."

Hmm…

You raise an eyebrow at Myrmidon Monk's words. Maybe he's not as bad a guy as he first sounded… Maybe. In any event, he hasn't said anything about Female Bishop's eyes.

You glance at Half-Elf Scout and finally see the edges of his lips turn up in a smile. "Eh, no need to act tough, I guess. We're a team, and they stole the words right out of my mouth."

Female Bishop takes her cue from this, saying "That's right" in a voice as quiet as a buzzing mosquito. "I admit I don't yet know…just how much I can do… But even so…"

Myrmidon Monk looks at the young woman, who attempts to face him despite her obvious fear, and clacks his mandibles uncomfortably. "…And what are you after?"

'After?' you parrot. He's changed the subject right out from under you.

"Money? Or perhaps…the wellspring of the Death that's said to lie in the deepest depths of the dungeon? I don't care either way, personally…"

You look around at the others.

'May I say what I think?'

"Fine by me," your cousin replies immediately, smiling. "Sis has got your back!"

Darn *second* cousin. You sigh. This is something about your cousin that you have unalloyed respect for. Half-Elf Scout grins, but beside him, Female Bishop doesn't seem quite sure what to focus on. "Um, you're speaking of challenging the labyrinth, yes?" she says.

"Y'know, you're right—we never talked about that," Female Warrior says with a grin of her own. "By the way, I'm after the money." But she probably knew that already.

You take a breath in, then let it out.

'*There's only one reason to go down there,*' you announce. You don't want to pretend that the whirlpool of money emerging from the dungeon holds no interest for you, but you have only one ultimate goal in delving the depths: to reach the lowest level and strike down the source of the Death.

"Do you mean that?" Female Bishop asks, blinking her unseeing eyes. "Is that really what you intend to do...?!" There are shades of joy in her voice—or so you think, but perhaps you're only imagining it.

You reply that of course you mean it. You don't know whether you'll reach your goal, but you intend to try.

"Heh-heh! That was *my* plan all along, even if the cap didn't want to go all the way down there. Who's worried about a little dungeon anyway?"

"Maybe the guy whose voice is shaking?" Female Warrior teases, her laughter pealing like a ringing bell.

"Hey, what's scary is scary!" Half-Elf Scout shoots back, his face stiff, but he's chuckling a little himself.

"I see— You are serious," Myrmidon Monk says with a long nod. "All right, I'm in."

'*You don't care that we're new to this?*'

"I did, but I changed my mind. I'm starting to wonder just who it is hiding down there at the bottom of that maze." Myrmidon Monk's mandibles clack together in a confidence-inspiring way.

That settles it, then. Your cousin, Half-Elf Scout, and you. Female Bishop, a former item identifier, a female warrior with no other harbor, and Myrmidon Monk. The six of you together are going to challenge the Dungeon of the Dead. In other words—this is the beginning of your adventure.

§

The Dungeon of the Dead sits on the edge of the fortress city, a great maw waiting for adventurers to enter. Those jaws have swallowed many brave souls who have come before you, and now they now wait like a looming monster.

The sun is past its zenith when you arrive, though it is still bright out. As soon as the light reaches the entrance of the dungeon, though, it seems to fail instantaneously, leaving only a stretch of darkness. The dungeon will show no secrets to those without the courage to take even a single step inside.

"So this is it… The Dungeon of the Dead…" Female Bishop's voice is a trembling whisper. She's more terrified than awed, but there's someone else whose voice is shaking even worse than hers.

"S-stop that. Actin' all scared, I mean. You're gonna start freaking me out, too…" It's Half-Elf Scout. He plays with the dagger at his belt, his fingers twitching.

You sigh in exasperation, and Female Warrior chuckles "Heh-heh" at almost the same time. "Don't worry," she says. "It's our job to look after the people behind us." You concur. If the enemies' blades—do they have blades? You don't know—reach your back row, you will already be lost.

The group hasn't talked too much about what you'll do down in the dungeon. Most of you only just met over the last few days, after all. Overly clever attempts at coordination aren't likely to get you much. At the very least, though, you decide to divide yourselves into front and back rows and try not to get in one another's way.

"But when we come back, everyone eats together!" your cousin reminds you with a grin that belies the gravity of the situation. Does she act that way on purpose? You're not sure. In any event, you need her. You nod, managing to only gently press your hand to your forehead. You'll let her choose what spells to use and when.

"Oh? I get to decide?"

You hate to admit it, but your cousin is the most experienced member of your party when it comes to magic. You'll be busy with your sword up front, so you think it might be best to let her handle matters in the rear. When you ask Myrmidon Monk if he's all right with this, he clacks out, "I don't care either way. I can come up front as well.

Which means, by process of elimination, you'll be handling the treasure chests, thief."

"Y-yeah, sure," Half-Elf Scout says. "But, uh, I'm a scout…"

"I don't really care what you are. What matters to me is that you don't run away even if it kills you. If you try to flee, I swear I'll hex you to death. I'll work for just about anything, but I won't work for free."

"Wh-whatever you say, man! Just remember I'm gonna put an end to this dungeon one of these days—don't underestimate me!"

You notice Female Bishop chuckling to herself at this exchange. You're all nervous. Yes, even you—but you think that's okay. Having decided so, you start toward the dungeon entrance.

The fortress city is built to enclose the mouth of the dungeon. It exists to prevent what is inside from getting out into the wider world, and an armed soldier is posted at the entrance. You bow politely to her—judging by the crest on her ample chest, she's a member of the royal guard—and reach for your porcelain rank tag.

"Oh, don't bother. We don't worry about ranks around here anymore," she says, waving her hand nonchalantly. She sounds downright cheerful. You keep one eye on her, but despite her relaxed tone, you don't see so much as an instant's lapse in her vigilance, and you realize just how much more powerful a member of the royal guard is than you. "The only things that count here are how far you've gotten in the dungeon, if you came back alive, and whether you keep coming back for more!"

"…Is it really that brutal?" Female Bishop asks in a voice strained with anxiety.

"Whatever you've heard, it's worse!" the guard replies. "Half the people who go in come running right back out—or die on their first visit."

'And the other half?'

"Eventually die exploring, I guess." The guard lets out a guffaw, then tosses five sacks at you. You ask her what they're for, to which she answers, "Body bags," her smile never faltering. "Five's plenty. A sixth wouldn't do you any good."

"No one to collect your corpses if you all die," you hear Female Warrior murmur from behind you, not sounding especially amused. It's just banter to this guard—you don't think she's trying to intimidate you. You frown. Anyway, if this is enough to scare you off, then you have no business in that dungeon. You aren't sure whether the gesture is on behalf of the nation or a bit of kindness from the guard herself...

"If you're scared, how about you go home? You must have families—well, not *must*, I guess."

The corners of your lips twist upward. You turn to your companions and ask, *'Onward?'* Your question is met with nods.

"It's all the same to me," Myrmidon Monk says. "If you won't go down there, I'll just find someone who will."

You shake your head and tell him there won't be any need for that, then indicate to the guard that there are no problems.

"Okay," she says, smiling at you. "You look like you gel together. That's not enough to keep you alive, but...

"Better than a party that doesn't get along."

You react to her whisper with an ambiguous expression. Do you, indeed, "gel"? You aren't sure. The only thing that will prove the matter one way or the other is when you come back alive from your dungeon crawl. You look around at the others one more time, then slowly take a step into the darkness of the dungeon. From behind you, the guard calls out, "Welcome to the proving ground!"

§

In front of you is the ladder you just climbed down, set into the rock face. As party leader, you have the job of making sure everyone gets back here in one piece. But then you notice something... You blink. The dungeon's shadows, uncommonly thick, veiling the world around you and making it hard even to breathe. You squint, but your eyes show no sign of adapting to the darkness; you can detect only a faint light. All you can see is a "wire frame," the barest outline of whatever looms around you in the dark.

"All right, just like we planned it," says Myrmidon Monk. "The warriors and me up front, the rest of you in back."

"Aye aye!"

Still, having someone with experience does make things go

smoother. As Myrmidon Monk instructs, Half-Elf Scout moves to the back row. You're glad it won't be just the two ladies there. You've heard it was the supernatural character of the space in this labyrinth that was the greatest obstacle to the soldiers who ventured here in serried ranks. That also accounts for why adventuring parties hardly, if ever, encounter one another in the depths.

The hallway is just wide enough for three to walk abreast, yet at the same time, it seems big enough for a dragon. Trying to keep track of ten people down here, or ten times that number, would be— No. You must think about your party's six people, including yourself. Your responsibility is great and lies heavily upon you.

"Hee-hee. We're counting on you, O leader." A soft hand adds itself to the weight on your shoulder, and a warm breath tickles your ear. You turn to see Female Warrior smiling at you. You respond with an affirmative grunt that comes out sounding stiff. But, well, you must admit she did help ease your anxiety a little bit.

Calmer now, you double-check your sword, making sure that it sits securely in its scabbard. It's a perfectly common item, not the work of some renowned master, but on this expedition, you're going to entrust your life to it. And not yours alone but those of your entire party: You would not want something to go wrong with it.

"Well, let's get going, then. Any direction will work. Let's see—how about…this way?" your cousin says.

"Oh, uh, um, wait a second…!" Female Bishop responds.

Blast your *second* cousin. You look at the ceiling, thanking your lucky stars for Female Bishop, who has stopped her. You really think that cousin of yours could do with just a little more anxiety. How nice it is to have trustworthy comrades.

"W-we'd better keep a map, or we'll get lost," Female Bishop says, sensitive to the fact that the rest of the party's eyes are suddenly on her. "Ahem, a-and in addition…" She blushes and looks at the ground, trailing off before she manages to pick up again. "The first crawl should only go as far as the first chamber…isn't that right?"

You reply that that's your plan. You glance at Female Warrior and Myrmidon Monk to make sure they agree.

"Get in, fight, find a treasure chest, get out. Simple," Female

Warrior responds with a snicker, but you don't find this a laughing matter. You saw with your own eyes what happened to her last party. But even ignoring that, it's obvious that surviving is no easy thing in this dungeon. You can hardly see what's in front of your face, and even the faint outlines continue only a short distance ahead. The trackless darkness of this labyrinth seems to swallow all light. You have no idea when a monster might appear or from where. You feel like you have your hands full just keeping track of your five companions. No wonder the army never returned from these depths.

You suddenly realize how tense your hand has become; you clench and unclench your fist to relax it. You think you finally see a frown on your cousin's face—assuming it isn't just the darkness playing tricks on you. The scolding you were about to give her dies on your lips, and you simply admonish her to be careful. Get in, get out. The debrief can be left for when it's over—and if you're all still alive. Now isn't the time.

"I have a little something here from a previous expedition," Myrmidon Monk says, digging noisily in his bag and coming up with a scroll of sheepskin paper. He unrolls it to reveal a map of the dungeon, if only the very smallest corner of it. Someone with a knowledge of scale has produced the map in a fine, carefully controlled hand.

"Hoo-wee," whistles Half-Elf Scout from beside you, clearly relieved. "Now, that's what I call bein' prepared, brother. Looks like you got this from the army or someplace. I've seen professional work that wasn't half as good as this."

Myrmidon Monk falls quiet for a moment; then his mandibles click as he says softly, "...It was me."

"You? You what?"

"I drew it."

"Heck..."

Well, you think, *we've all just met*. There's a lot you don't know about one another.

Female Bishop, meanwhile, reaches out hesitantly. You look at her in puzzlement, but your cousin quickly grasps what she wants and passes her the map. "Here you go!"

"Th-thank you very much," Female Bishop says, exhaling audibly and running her fingers over the map almost in a caress.

"Can you read it?" Myrmidon Monk asks, and Female Bishop replies that she can, continuing to feel the sheepskin under her fingers.

"I'm not quite completely blind to begin with... Anyway, I can feel the difference between the ink and the paper."

"I see," Myrmidon Monk replies. "In darkness like this, I guess it doesn't matter how good your vision is anyway."

That causes you to smile and nod, and after a moment's thought, you suggest that Female Bishop be entrusted with taking care of the map.

"What...?" she says, looking at you in surprise. "Me?"

There would obviously be some hurdles for anyone on the front line trying to map the dungeon and take care of business at the same time. In the rear, you want your scout to be paying attention, and as for your cousin...well. She's your cousin.

"...I get the feeling my little brother insulted me just now!" your *second* cousin says hotly, though you tried to make it sound like you were joking. In any case, you don't think she really means it. She's just trying to break the tension that's making her so stiff. Even if she didn't mean it, the effect is to relax everyone, not actually to chide you.

"Consider it a kind turn from the captain—he wants you to focus on your magic!" Half-Elf Scout says—it's almost as if he can read your mind already. You nod for effect.

Female Bishop, listening to this back-and-forth, finally clenches her fist. "U-um, I-I'll give it everything I can."

You acknowledge her dedication. You doubt someone with such an evident sense of responsibility as she has would make any careless mistakes—especially not while inside this dungeon. As Myrmidon Monk said moments ago, the best way not to get lost seems to be not to rely on your eyes. And more than anything...

"Er, I'll borrow the map, then."

"Mm. Ah, do you have a pencil? Or charcoal—that's fine, too."

"Oh, good point. I'm sorry... Might I borrow some?" Female Bishop says. She seems almost excited as she opens up the map and prepares to draw. It looks like this is having a positive effect on her, helping to reverse the gloom of her former mistakes and her time as an identifier.

"Just a thought—for if we survive," Female Warrior whispers to you with a glance. "But I like a man who knows how to be considerate."

You pass off the tease with a smile, then peer once more into the darkness of the dungeon. You won't get anywhere just standing here at the entrance. You feel you've already spent too much time talking. Preparation is crucial—but could it be that fear of the labyrinth will seize you before you realize it?

You shake your head slowly, then take a deliberate step forward.

'Let's go.'

Everyone follows you silently.

§

You suck in a breath. Or is it you being sucked in with every step you take? You don't think you've gone very far, yet if you were to turn around, you know for a fact the light from the surface would no longer be visible. There would be only the hazy outlines of the hallway extending away from you, until even that is covered completely by the darkness.

The path in front of you is no different. You could almost feel as if you were all alone here in the gloom. Is it the dank murk pervading the dungeon that makes you feel this way or perhaps the assumption that monsters await you ahead? Maybe both.

If nothing else, you grasp now why parties so rarely run into one another down here. In the dungeon, people are alone. The only things you can rely on are your own strength and your companions, your party members. You're in the realm of the Non-Prayers now. You have a distinct feeling that even if you set off running back the way you came right now, there would still be no guarantee you would reach the surface alive. You see why a journey into the dungeon—even just one—produces such a distinction among adventurers: those who have done it and those who haven't.

"Don't tell me you're scared," Female Warrior says from right next to your ear, letting out that ringing laugh. You shake your head no. You ask the others if they're all right and receive yeses and uh-huhs with varying degrees of tension in their voices.

No answer from Female Bishop.

Hmm? You look in her direction to find she's concentrating on the sheepskin map, her pencil working furiously. She has the previous work for reference, and you've been traveling in a straight line—it would be difficult to make a mistake. You reiterate the question about whether she's all right, and your cousin adds, "Hey," finally eliciting a high-pitched "Oh, y-yes" from Female Bishop. "S-sorry, I was so engrossed..."

You shake your head again. *'It's fine.'* Certainly better than freezing up with fear.

Quite suddenly, your cousin says: "In the chamber, I wonder... I wonder what kind of monsters we'll find."

"Could be anything," Myrmidon Monk responds. "On the first floor, small humanoids are common. And some who resemble adventurers themselves. Other than that...well, money, I suppose."

"Money?"

"Don't ask me why. But some of the guys who hole up in those chambers instead of wandering the hallways have treasure chests with them."

Hack and slash: It's the classic adventurer job. So you find your interest piqued more than anything by the mention of "some who resemble adventurers themselves." It was supposed to be monsters down here. Do adventurers ever attack other adventurers?

"I don't exactly know," Female Warrior says. "But...there's thieves. Or like...dead people who've lost their souls, I think?" Her voice is harsher now, with no trace of the lightheartedness you heard when she was teasing you. You simply ask if they're powerful. "These creatures that are like adventurers... Maybe they really are adventurers. But they're pretty—well..." She trails off but nods at you nonetheless. You can just hear her whisper: "If any of them show up, we have to run." Otherwise those five body bags threaten to come in handy.

You let out a long breath. No point being nervous before a fight actually starts—but the time to worry about that is over.

Before you stands the door of a chamber, shut fast.

"L-looks like this is it," Half-Elf Scout says, swinging his arms to loosen up his stiff body. "Gotta say, if I were the Dungeon Master, I wouldn't put any loot right on the first floor, but..."

"Whoever's in there and whatever we get from them, we need to take them out in one shot. We don't have the cash to show up at the temple." Myrmidon Monk confirms your tactics in a casual, almost mechanical tone. You nod at him. It's just like you discussed on the way here. "Then there are just three things to do: bust in there, kill them, and get home."

"So you're saying we go in with spells blazing!" your cousin says excitedly.

To which Myrmidon Monk eventually mutters, "...In a word, yes."

You have no objection to this. There may come a time when you must avoid consuming your spells, even if it makes things more difficult for you in the short term, but that time is not now. The only things you should be thinking about at this moment are fighting, surviving, and getting home. Fight and win—that's the first challenge.

"Heh-heh-heh. I'm ready anytime. Are you?" Female Warrior says, hefting her spear. Female Bishop quickly rolls up the map, grips the sword and scales in hand, and nods. You likewise draw your sword, checking all the rivets, rubbing a bit of spit onto the scabbard to lubricate it.

You indicate to the others that now is the moment, then raise your foot—and kick in the door.

"_____?!"

When you and your party burst into the chamber, the monsters crouching in the shadows look up in surprise. Five of them!

"All right! Small humanoids, none of the adventurer-like ones!" Myrmidon Monk calls. In the gloom, you can't quite see what you're actually facing. And although the enemies aren't especially strong, there are five of them. They already outnumber your front row. In light of their number, you promptly instruct your cousin to use a spell.

"Y-yeah, sure, coming right up...!" she replies, her voice tight. "The three of us will coordinate!"

But there's no answer from Female Bishop. She's gone stiff, and her breath seems caught in her throat. You give a small shake of your head, using your free hand, the one not holding your sword, to form the sigil for Sleep. When your cousin sees you, she waves her staff, loudly chanting words of true power. "*Sagitta...quelta...raedius!* Strike home, arrow!"

Instantaneously, white mist gathers around the battlefield only to be pierced by arrows of light that fly forth at the girl's command. Magic Missile is a very basic spell; even you know it. Although it's not especially powerful, it always finds its target, and in this situation, that's a comforting thought.

"GROORBB?!"

"GORB?! GBBOROB?!"

The monsters, first disoriented by the fog and then struck by a rain of arrows, cry out, but...

"I hit them! So why—?" Your cousin sounds disbelieving. There are still five opponents standing. Her Magic Missile isn't enough to make up the difference in strength. But you don't care. You grip the hilt of your sword with both hands and raise it high, calling out to the other two in the front row.

"We're good; it's not as if they're invincible... Let's go!" Myrmidon Monk says.

"Aha, now *this* is what gets my blood pumping!" Female Warrior crows.

You shout back at them, then plunge into the middle of the enemy formation, your sword working furiously.

"GOORB!"

"GBBGORO!!"

You aim at the figure standing at the head of the enemy group. You bring your sword down in a tremendous chop before the creature fully processes what's going on.

"GOOBOGR?!"

Powered by the momentum of your advance, the blow cleaves the monster from shoulder to abdomen, shattering its collarbone and spilling its entrails on the ground. The monster's small size makes this a bit of overkill, but at least it did the job. You follow through, pulling your blade out and flicking off the blood before sliding forward, finding your footing. You look for the next enemy. Four remain...

"GOBB!"

"Ahhh! Ow, that hurts!"

"GOOBOBRRRB?!"

"Nasty little—"

Make that two.

Your party members are already engaged. Female Warrior deflects an enemy's dagger against her leather armor, then forces the creature back by thrusting with the butt of her spear. The enemy is small. As with the problem you had modulating your force a moment ago, Female Warrior is struggling to keep the appropriate fighting distance. Myrmidon Monk, meanwhile, is wielding an ax-like shortsword in a reverse grip, parrying enemy attacks with precise movements. These opponents would not be remotely fearsome in a one-on-one contest, but their numbers have the power to turn the tide.

"GGGOBOO!!"

"GOORBG?!"

It's up to you to hold off the remaining foes while your companions deal with their current engagements.

"Want me to take one of 'em off your hands, Cap?" Half-Elf Scout calls out, but you shake your head and face the two creatures in front of you.

"GGGBOOROGB!"

"GOORBG!"

One of them slowly approaches you with a crude club in hand, paying no special attention to distancing. The monster doesn't seem to be thinking about its comrade at all, except possibly as a tool for ensuring its own survival. Ugly and selfish—you've heard stories about these creatures. There's no question now what you're dealing with.

Goblins!

"Hee...heek...!" Female Bishop suppresses a shriek behind you. In the instant you're distracted, the goblins rush at you. One from each side simultaneously. You deflect the club from the right with your katana and simply accept the blow from your left with your armor. You can hear the sound of the gnarled tree branch the monster is holding as it slaps against your side.

"——!" You hear your cousin shout, but you ignore her. It's all right. There's a dull pain, but it isn't critical. It's getting hard to catch your breath. Your legs feel like they might collapse at any moment, but you order them to stay firm. If you so much as slip, you might as well tumble right into one of those body bags. Or your back row may become exposed, or you leave the others on the front vulnerable to attack. You strengthen your grip, intending to cut your way through the goblins facing you, but something doesn't feel right.

"GOORGB!!"

The blade of your sword is half-buried in the goblin's club!

You put too much force into the exchange. The goblin with the club cackles, and out of the corner of your eye, you can see the one on your left raise its weapon. You strengthen your grip on your sword like a mortal game of tug-of-war, then force your arms down as if chopping wood.

"GOROO?!"

The two halves of the club tumble through the air. You have one clear advantage: sheer physical strength. And your sword is more than a match for some goblin's stick. Your ready your blade as the goblin on the right stumbles as if pushed. Without missing a beat, you take a high stance, then step to the left after wrapping both hands around your sword.

"GBBBOBOG?! GOROGB?!"

It seems that the goblin hoping to follow up by crushing your skull never imagined it might become your target. With its branch still raised, it's split clean down the middle, then collapses faceup. A spray of revolting blood drenches you. Now covered in gore, you position your sword in a low stance, then advance, meaning to slice the final goblin from below...

"Aha! This one's—mine!"

"GBBBOORG?!"

There's a *thump*, and the goblin suddenly has a spear growing out of its chest. It collapses to the floor, still twitching, and Female Warrior strides over and extracts her weapon. Sopping with blood, she licks a bit of the stuff off her cheek. "That makes two... Right?" When she smiles, her lips are as red as if she'd put on lip rouge. You heave a sigh and nod.

You ask Myrmidon Monk how it's going for him, and he responds, "I'm done over here. Well, they were just goblins. Of course we managed."

The ax-like weapon must be sharper than it looks. Myrmidon Monk has sliced one of the monsters' heads clean off. You glance behind you, and Half-Elf Scout waves a hand without a word. Your cousin is pale, but— Hold on. Your gaze settles on Female Bishop, trembling uncontrollably. You ask if she's all right, and she says, "H— Y-yes... I'm...f-f-fine... Safe..." But she doesn't seem completely there.

Now you look at your cousin, who shakes her head vigorously; you nod to say you'll entrust this to her.

Let's take her at her word.

You let out a slow breath. You lean on your katana like a walking stick as fatigue suddenly washes over you. Now that it's finished, you realize how brief the confrontation was... But maybe it's safe to say you passed the first trial. Notwithstanding the fact that one or two of you have a bit of experience, you're effectively a party of six novices. Together, you confronted five monsters who made their home here on the uppermost level of the dungeon. Perhaps your two groups could be considered roughly equal in strength.

The battle you just fought would get nothing but a chuckle from more established adventurers, but for you it was a matter of life and death. For a moment, none of you say anything as you contemplate the outcome. In the chamber, rank with the smell of mold and now with blood and death, there is only the sound of the six of you steadying your breathing.

There were more enemies than you expected, and one wrong move would have meant a baptism with the Death. Little if anything separates you from the goblins lying dead at your feet. You and the others are so exhausted, you practically forget to tend to your own wounds.

"All riiiight! We did it!"

Half-Elf Scout lets out a victory whoop seemingly meant to clear the heavy air. You feel the tension snap like a thread, and everyone looks at one another. You let out a breath, wipe the blood from your katana with a piece of rice paper, and return it to its scabbard.

As many blows as you struck, the sword remained strong. You owe your life to this weapon now.

"Yo, Captain, great work there! Come on, everyone—let's have a drink and catch our breath."

You take the proffered canteen and then take a draft. The lukewarm water feels piercingly cold to you, refreshing.

"I-I'm sorry. I just…"

Half-Elf Scout passes off Female Bishop's tiny-voiced apology by pulling the canteen from her bag. "Don't mention it—just drink. I ain't one to talk either way; I hardly moved myself!"

She accepts the canteen, her hands shaking visibly, the water spilling as she pours it down her throat. As if to follow her lead, everyone else takes out their water and wets their throats. You nod at Half-Elf Scout discreetly so that Female Bishop doesn't see you.

'It's not common for scouts or thieves in the back row to participate in combat.'

He therefore exerted the least energy of all of you, and it's your good fortune that he's able to use that store of stamina to be thoughtful like this.

"Like I said, don't mention it. Nothing special." Half-Elf Scout waves away your remark, the joints of his fingers cracking. It's true: His battle is only about to begin. Almost magically, a blood-streaked treasure chest appears, sitting there as if unconcerned. Had the goblins squirreled it away, or had it always been in this room?

"You think we're the first people to come in here…?" asks your cousin, who has appeared at your side, still pale with the last vestiges of fear and tension. You shake your head: You don't know, either. This room is right near the dungeon entrance. You doubt you're the first party to come by.

"I don't know how it works, either. They say the chests just appear." Myrmidon Monk crouches down, almost audibly, in the corner of the room. "Maybe it's just the way the dungeon is, or maybe the master set it up this way. Frankly, I don't care which. In the end, it means an endless supply of money and treasure for us."

Ah. You nod your understanding, but somehow you feel a chill; you close your eyes.

"Hey, if you're tired, let me hit you with a miracle. Don't want to screw this up just because you didn't get enough rest."

"Aw, I think I'll manage… Emphasis on *'think,'*" Half-Elf Scout says.

"Hee-hee." Female Warrior snickers in that teasing way of hers. "If you do screw up, then it's on you."

"Erk…"

"H-hang tough, okay?" your cousin urges.

Half-Elf Scout grunts, "Yeah."

From Female Bishop there are no words, and the voices die down, leaving only the scraping of your scout pulling out a set of seven tools.

Listening to this all happening in the dim gloom, you begin to examine the shadow that seems to have fallen upon your heart. It feels like the Death itself is beckoning to you.

You think of this treasure, apparently worth risking your life for. The mysteries that lie at the heart of all these dangers. The dungeon depths, crawling with monsters... Who could withstand them all? And how much death would there be before someone finally did? You see now that the darkness of this dungeon is none other than the darkness of the Death...

"...I'm guessin' this thing's rigged with some kinda trap..."

Click, click.

When you open your eyes, Half-Elf Scout's fingers are working dexterously, the tool in his hand searching the keyhole. He has several long picks and needles and a thin, flat dagger that looks like a chisel. He inspects the keyhole, then slides the blade of the chisel in between the lid and the body of the chest, patiently feeling things out. You understand that he's checking for traps and then attempting to undo the lock, but you don't know exactly what processes are involved. The most you can do to help is to stay out of his way.

Which isn't to say you can simply rest on your heels—traps come in many varieties. There could be an explosion that wipes your party out, or an alarm that brings more monsters running, or you could be teleported to gods know where... Your job at this moment is to stand beside him, ready for whatever might happen—the exact opposite of the situation a few minutes ago.

It's agonizing to be unable to do anything but stand and wait.

"Hey... About the girl..." In the midst of this anxiety, Female Warrior whispers to you. Her gore-stained cheeks look faintly flushed—is it simply the last traces of blood from when she tried to wipe off the cruor, or is it the leftover excitement of battle?

The girl? You cock your head, and she jerks her chin toward a corner of the room. You see your cousin gently patting Female Bishop on the back, offering her water.

"Don't be too angry with her, okay?" Female Warrior says. "Sounds like she's been through a lot." She casts her eyes slightly downward and knits her brow.

As nonchalantly as you can, you ask whether she's done anything worthy of getting upset.

Female Warrior looks taken aback for a second, but then the edges of her eyes soften. "Good point… Yeah, it must've been my imagination. Sorry to bother you, huh?"

You tell her again that there's nothing to apologize for and then return your attention to the treasure chest.

Everyone has their own life story, their own feelings. Unless and until they want to talk about them, want someone else to listen to them, then it's nobody's business to go nosing around in them. Female Bishop isn't the only one: The same is true of your cousin and even the female warrior with a number for a name. That's why you don't say anything further, just focus on preparing for anything unfortunate that might happen.

She doesn't say anything, either. Nor does anyone else.

A moment later, you hear the *thunk* of the chest's lid falling open, and Half-Elf Scout bounces to his feet. "Wh-whoa…!" Sounds like a trap to you. You put a hand on your katana, ready for anything. But Half-Elf Scout turns to you, and his face relaxes. "I freakin' got the freakin' thing! It freakin' opened!"

"Aw, I knew you could do it!" Female Warrior's concern vanishes in an instant, replaced by a mewl like a coquettish kitten as she slides over toward Half-Elf Scout. Myrmidon Monk gets to his feet with interest, and your cousin, her face shining, leads Female Bishop over by the hand. The gold coins Half-Elf Scout pulls out of the chest glitter brightly.

You let out a deep breath.

§

It simply isn't possible to tell who, in the now ever so slightly more relaxed atmosphere, suggests going back. One by one you turn, Half-Elf Scout taking a last look in the chest to make sure it's cleared out, and then you leave the chamber behind. Your feet—they feel light, somehow, and heavy at the same time. It's a strange feeling for you.

There's still a haze of fatigue and anxiety, but relief and even joy pound in your chest.

You survived.

You won.

Just against a few goblins, yes, but you've taken your first steps into the dungeon.

"Man, oh man… We got a nice haul out of that," Half-Elf Scout says. He's carrying the money; you figure it will be best to split it up later. When you gathered together all the gold coins—finding a few silver ones mixed in as well—you found they filled one sack to bulging. Enough to weigh a person down on the road home and a considerable supply of resources for each of you, even split six ways.

One score, and you've already made it big. No wonder there's no end of people who dream of becoming adventurers to make a real living.

"I could go back home right now and live in the lap of luxury for a year on this!"

"Going to skedaddle with an armful of chump change?" Myrmidon Monk asks, turning a cold compound eye on Half-Elf Scout. "Fine by me. Whatever makes you happy."

"Whoa there…" It's hard to say how serious the intimidating-sounding bugman is. Half-Elf Scout raises a hand in surrender. "Just jokin'," he says, provoking a giggle from Female Warrior beside you.

"Money matters, you know?" she says, almost in a whisper. "Nothing comes cheap around here." Not food, not pleasure, and certainly not the equipment that keeps you alive.

The presence of adventurers, who make their livings just the way their name implies, drives up the price of everything in the fortress city. People frequently remark that the cheapest thing in town is an adventurer's life.

Female Warrior shakes her head when you mention this, though. "Not true," she says, her hair rippling with the motion of her head. "Around here, even life has its price. Unless you die, of course…"

Apparently, anything and everything is expensive. You sigh.

"I wonder, though—what country is this money from?" Your cousin is industriously examining the treasure, which you declined to inspect first. The darkness doesn't make it easy, but she said she was curious. "I've never seen anything like it. These gold coins are definitely old, though."

Many a nation has risen and fallen in the Four-Cornered World since the Age of the Gods. That is nothing new. And if these coins seem strange, well, the dungeon is a strange place. You cast your gaze around, following the hall as it drifts into view. This aspect of the dungeon seemed bizarre when you came in, yet now, on the way back, you're already growing accustomed to it. You seem to recall the access to the surface isn't too far away...

"...U-um..." As you turn around to ask for a look at the map, there's an uneasy voice behind you. It's Female Bishop. Surprised to have inadvertently spoken up the same moment you were turning toward her, she stumbles over herself before finally mumbling, "It's nothing."

Your cousin puts an encouraging hand on her back. "It's all right. Speak up," she says softly. "If my little brother is mean to you, I'll be sure to give him a good talking-to later."

You inform them in no uncertain terms that she's your *second* cousin, to which Half-Elf Scout responds simply, "I guess he's at that rebellious age."

You make a point of looking annoyed. Then Myrmidon Monk says, "Makes no difference. If you have something to say, then say it. You don't want to talk, don't."

"..." Female Bishop looks at the ground, not speaking right away under the sharp words.

"Which is it?" Myrmidon Monk asks bluntly.

"I... I'm sorry," she finally says. "About earlier. Ahem... I..."

Her voice is shaking terribly; it sounds tiny and uncertain, like a child about to be punished.

Well, now. You nod seriously. And then wonder aloud what she could possibly be talking about.

"Pfff..." Female Warrior claps a hand to her mouth as if pretending she didn't mean to laugh, her shoulders shaking. Hardly able to suppress her laughter, she shoots you an accusing look. You shake your head as though you can't imagine what Female Bishop could have in mind. There was nothing critical anyway.

Female Bishop, detecting Female Warrior's snickering, shakes her head in confusion.

"Yeah, don't sweat it. We won the day in a big way," Half-Elf Scout reassures her with a firm nod.

Myrmidon Monk lets a hiss of air out between his mandibles, muttering, "Is that all you had to say?"

"There, see?" your cousin says, patting Female Bishop on the back.

"Yes," she replies, her voice still small. "Um... When we get back. To the surface, I mean. Would you be so kind as to look at the map for me? I'd like...someone to check my work..." *Because I'll keep working on it. Next time, I promise, nothing like this will...* Such seemed to be what she was trying to imply.

You have no objection, of course. This is an important matter. When you say as much, her face relaxes. Maybe it's just you, but you think the "Right!" with which she responds sounds positively excited.

"Ooh, look who's scoring points with the ladies," Female Warrior says, jabbing you in the side as if to say, *This is payback for earlier.*

Shortly thereafter, you spot the ladder to the surface. Your adventure, your first attempt at exploration, has ended in success. Now you just have to go home.

It's nobody's fault, what happens next.

In the darkness, you feel something sticky underfoot.

§

"Look who's here," Female Warrior whispers, letting out a breath, then squinting into the darkness. Myrmidon Monk doesn't say anything at all, his antennae working as he draws his short blade. Your companions in the back row stop as well.

"...What is it?" your cousin asks, but you don't answer, just put your hand on your sword and slowly draw. The wire-frame depths of the maze emit a hideous, watery noise. You think you can count the sounds coming closer—one, two, three, four, five...six.

At first, you take them for blood-flecked vomit. Like squirming, translucent organs—but alive. The globs of red-black goop quiver in front of your party.

"The heck are those?!" Half-Elf Scout cries.

"Slimes," Myrmidon Monk replies. "No telling what they'll do. Watch yourselves."

"Oh, I'm watching, but… Ugh. The way they *quiver*…" Female Warrior looks disturbed as she stands there with her spear at the ready, and you can't blame her. From the back row, Female Bishop and your cousin both stifle cries of what you assume is disgust.

"I wonder if S-Sleep would work on them…," your cousin mumbles, clutching her short staff in front of her large chest. You don't know any better than she does. None of you has much magic left, and you're uneasy with what might happen if you flail aimlessly.

"Slimes…," Female Bishop utters as if testing the word in her mouth. "What should I do?"

We shouldn't use our spells.

You hesitate for a moment after the thought occurs to you, then voice it to your party.

"What?!" your cousin says, but you repeat the instruction. You inform the party that magic is your trump card, to be used when the sword proves ineffective. "Got it!" your cousin responds.

"I'll get ready as well," Female Bishop adds, sounding tense, and then you start to close in on the wriggling creatures carefully.

You've got plenty of practice slicing at humanoid creatures, but living slimes? You don't know how to deliver the cut or where.

"…Careful," Myrmidon Monk says again. "I hear slimes are poisonous and can eat away at weaponry. Guess we've got no choice but to kill them regardless." He, too, is approaching the slimes with incredible caution.

Even as you get closer, the monsters just sit there quivering; they don't look like they're about to spring at you. It's very unsettling, you think, as you spit on the hilt of your sword and slowly grasp it with both hands.

"Make sure to try to minimize splatter," Female Warrior murmurs, and you nod, bringing your katana up in a sweep from a low position.

The blade slices upward easily, as if passing through water, and emerges on the other side with a *ploop*. The slime is cut clean in two, the halves spreading on the floor of the hallway, staining it dark. You feel like you've just cut through a soaked bundle of grass. You wouldn't want to accidentally slam your sword against the floor, but even so, this might turn out to be easier than you expected.

You feel a little bad for your cousin, who looks so eager with her staff at the ready, but it's good news for your party if your katana can settle this.

"Ooh! That's one down! These guys aren't so tough…!" Myrmidon Monk has his knife in his hand like he's going to dissect an animal; he stabs at a monster. The blade arcs languidly into the slime, ending the creature's life.

"Yeah, compared with those goblins earlier, these things aren't so scary… I guess?" Female Warrior nimbly swings around the haft of her spear, almost scooping one of the slimes off the ground with the point. It flies through the air and slams against the wall, spattering across it like some fancy new style of painting. It bursts like an exploding fruit, but Female Warrior seems unfazed. You grumble something about the warning she gave you earlier, but she just giggles.

There's nothing special to say about how the rest of the fight goes. Female Warrior, Myrmidon Monk, and you make the most of your weapons to annihilate the slimes. There are some reddish sprays like blood, but nothing about them seems poisonous or acidic—just sticky. Still, they're too weird to simply walk by, so you have to engage them. At length, you discover there are no more piles of goo worthy of the name, and you stand there in the hallway, breathing heavily.

"Over already…?" Female Warrior says, leaning against her spear as she catches her breath. You can hear the harsh *huff, puff* of her panting, no doubt exacerbated by the earlier battle. As for you, you're still holding up under the succession of fights. Although you wouldn't mind being able to lean against the wall, if only it wasn't covered in slime.

"Phew. No way of telling how many of them there were, now…" Myrmidon Monk's mandibles clack together as he wipes his dagger on the sleeve of his robe. As he says, the whole floor is covered in reddish liquid, like a sea of blood. That's all that's left of the creatures that squirmed and writhed until moments before. They're too primitive to call living creatures, and you don't feel that you *killed* them, although the fatigue remains.

"Four or five of 'em, I'd say... Anybody count?"

"But I heard six different things crawling toward us," Female Bishop says hesitantly, looking around with her sightless eyes. You, wearing a puzzled expression, nudge the ocean of goop with the tip of your sword. You thought there were six as well, but there's no sign of movement, and you figure it's safe to assume they're all gone.

"Guess it doesn't matter..."

"It certainly does," your cousin retorts, puffing out her cheeks. "I didn't have a chance to use my trump card!"

"Hey, if that's what's bothering you, I didn't exactly get a chance to shine, either," Half-Elf Scout says, trying to talk her down. "They didn't even cough up a treasure chest." He pulls a canteen from his baggage. Taking his cue, you flick the filth from your sword and return it to its scabbard, then dig through your items. Out comes the stopper: one mouthful, two. The lukewarm water feels wonderful on your dry throat.

Again: It's no one's fault.

You're all tired from the battle; you're feeling relaxed. It's hard to shift gears straight back to vigilance in preparation for another fight. Doing so won't cure your fatigue, either. Not by a long shot. Not to mention, the monsters that appeared were slimes, weak-looking creatures that seem to go down in one hit. It would be ungenerous to refer to the relief you and your party felt as arrogance or even a lapse of judgment.

So there's no one to blame for this. But if someone had to, then maybe...

"Ngha?!"

One might say it was you who failed, failed to notice the red slime creeping up the wall.

By the time you hear the scream, it's too late. You turn around, still holding your canteen, to discover Female Warrior's head has disappeared. Her beautiful face is completely covered by the slime that dropped from the ceiling.

"Hrn...! Hrn, hngh, hnnn, hrrrnnngh?!" Muted screams are

accompanied by a panoply of small bubbles. Female Warrior collapses to the floor, writhing in the ocean of slime as she tears at her face. You try to pull the slime off her, but she's kicking her long legs, and she nails you right in the stomach.

But you can't just leave her to her own devices. She's clearly desperate. Even as her entire body becomes covered in slime, she continues to resist.

"Shit—she's going to drown!" Myrmidon Monk says, his tone urgent, and between the two of you, you manage to restrain the flailing woman.

So this is what it means to drown on dry land. That's what the slime is trying to do to Female Warrior, to drown her without any water. You shouldn't have let yourself forget that it's goblins, not slimes, that are the weakest monsters. Slimes, given the slightest chance, will drop onto a foe's face like this, stop their breathing, and then consume them.

"Grab that dagger of yours and cut the damn thing off!" Myrmidon Monk commands.

"Hold on! I don't know if I can do it without cutting her face!" Half-Elf Scout shouts back.

"It's better than dying!"

"Damn these vicious things…!" Half-Elf Scout approaches uncertainly with his dagger in hand, but the slime is so slippery, he can't find any purchase. No matter how nimble his fingers, the goo just slips away.

You're desperately attempting to calm Female Warrior down; you try to keep a hold on her ankles, but in the process you get kicked in the ribs several more times. Finally, you lie across them; you can feel her feet kicking slightly under you.

"Hrn… Hn, hnnngh…?!" You feel her movements getting weaker and weaker, though; you can tell all too clearly the strength is leaving her. Her life is ebbing away. You can't let this go on. But you're not having any bright ideas. All you feel is panic. You have to do something, quickly…

"That's it…! I've got it!"

You hardly hear your cousin whisper to Female Bishop. Female

Bishop responds with a look of confusion, but then her mouth tightens, and she rushes over to you.

"Hrm? What is it…?" Myrmidon Monk asks.

"Pardon me. I'll have to explain later…" She all but ignores him, kneeling next to the squirming Female Warrior. She reaches one hand out toward the woman's face and puts the other to her own delicate chest as if in prayer.

"Inflammarae… Inflammarae… Inflammarae!"

Licking tongues of flame appear. Birthed by her words of true power, they spread to the slime in the blink of an eye.

"?!?!?!" The lump of goo cries out, but Half-Elf Scout's hand is already moving.

"Now!" Heedless of the flames, he grabs the slime and slashes it with his blade. There's a wet smack, and the creature explodes from the inside out in a burst of red muck. It apparently lost the ability to hold itself together. Now it's no different from its comrades.

"How is she? Is she alive…?!" Myrmidon Monk peers at Female Warrior, and you likewise lean over her. Her face is pale, bloodless, and her hair is splayed every which way, stuck to her cheeks. Her eyes are open, though, and her mouth gasps at the air like a fish on dry land.

"Ah…aiee…ah…"

She can't breathe.

The moment you realize, you pull her up into a sitting position and slap her hard on the back.

"Ugh…ghhh—hrgh!" A bit of slime that had worked its way down her throat comes flying back out of her mouth. *"Cough…hack!* Ugh… Ergh…"

The red glop hits the floor with an unpleasant smack. Female Warrior sucks in air even as she spits out more bits of slime that got inside her. You rub her back as she crouches there, weeping and vomiting. Touching her, you find she feels small and delicate; she's trembling so hard, you fear she might shake herself apart, but she is unquestionably alive.

You let out a deep breath.

"I know a spell of magical fire," Female Bishop says quietly into the silence. She keeps clenching and unclenching the hand that produced the flame, as if unable to believe what she's done. "And we thought it might be possible to burn the thing away with that word. It was her idea…"

"Sure glad it worked," your cousin says with a bit of a smile.

"Me too," comes Female Bishop's soft response.

Your cousin eases her way over to Female Warrior, offering a canteen. "Sorry my brother's so thoughtless. Here."

You decide to let it go this time. Pointedly not correcting your cousin, you move over so that she can sit next to Female Warrior. You're surprised, then, to feel a tug on your arm. You find Female Warrior's weak hands clutching your sleeve. "…I…s…rry…"

You shake your head, taking her trembling hand in yours and placing it on the waterskin. Female Warrior rinses her mouth and spits several times. You lean against the wall—you don't care whether it's slimy anymore—and edge your way over toward Female Bishop.

No, there is nothing in particular to apologize for. If anything, you mumble, it's you yourself who should say you're sorry.

Female Bishop looks surprised for a moment, then gently shakes her head. "I don't think so…" Her tense face relaxes somewhat; her voice is still soft but firmer now. "In fact, I'm sure I don't know what you're talking about."

§

When you emerge from the gloomy mouth of the dungeon, a gentle, cool breeze brushes your cheek. It's the air of night. You look up to see stars in the sky, shimmering lights against a field of black like so much spilled ink. In the distance are other lights coming from the town. The fortress city shines brightly, blending into the starry sky. You can see a curl of smoke rising lazily in the distance, illuminated by the town lights; it's the volcano where a dragon is said to live.

"Finally…made it…" Half-Elf Scout sounds downright exhausted. You have no idea how long you were underground. You can't help thinking the road home feels much harder than the road here was. The fact that you're still alive to breathe the air of the surface once more is only because the pips of the dice smiled on you.

You look around at the others, checking if they're all okay, particularly putting a hand on Female Warrior, who's leaning against you for support. "Heh. Just fine…," she responds, but her words are few and weak.

After the encounter with the slimes, she received healing from Female Bishop and Myrmidon Monk, but it will take time for her stamina to recover. She's still pale, her body obviously leaden. Despite the muscles evident on her arms, her limbs look soft and uncertain with her so drained of strength.

You acknowledge her answer with a nod, then suggest you start out by looking for an inn. The debrief can wait till tomorrow.

"Don't much care what we do," Myrmidon Monk says promptly. He clacks his mandibles together. "I'm not so soft as to be all that tired. If you said you wanted to go out for a drink, I'd be game."

"As for me, I…I guess I am a bit tired," your cousin says, pressing a hand to her cheek and making no effort to hide the exhaustion in her voice, no doubt out of consideration for Female Warrior. "What do you think we should do?"

"Wha—?" Female Bishop is taken aback. Apparently, she didn't expect the conversation to turn to her. "Well, uh, let's see…" She puts a finger to her pretty lips, glancing hesitantly from you to Female Warrior and back, then says, "I'd like to have a good talk with everyone, but…I think it might be best to do it tomorrow."

"Well, that settles it, then," Half-Elf Scout interrupts before Female Warrior can say anything—she looks like she's about to try to put on a strong front. You smile and agree, though you think you hear someone grumble "Hmph!" Your imagination, surely.

The sentinel from the knights' royal guard watches you go as you head back toward town, everyone in the party leaning on everyone else. She makes no particular comment about the fact that you're still alive. After all, if she did, you might not come back the next time. So you say nothing yourself. You simply focus on putting one foot in front of the other.

Before long, you reach the city limits, and the bustle of the streets greets your ears. You're almost overwhelmed, but this is perfectly normal; it's the dungeon that is impossibly quiet. That's what makes the people sound so loud.

"We're...back," your cousin says quietly. You nod. The fact is only just now sinking in for you.

'It seems outrageously noisy up here.'

"True that. Almost looks like there's a festival or something," Half-Elf Scout remarks.

"I don't seem to remember tonight being anything special..." Female Bishop sounds uncertain. "But then again, I can't be sure. There's no telling how long we were down in that dungeon."

"Doesn't matter," Myrmidon Monk says flatly. "If you want to head back to the inn, then let's get going."

Of course. You make sure Female Warrior is leaning safely against you as you wade into the crowd and make for your inn.

Most places adventurers stay are located above a tavern. This traditional arrangement has persisted even after the emergence of the so-called Adventurers Guilds. The one here in the fortress city is very much in the classic style, tavern below and inn above.

As you retrace the steps you took to get to the dungeon, you notice something is different from when you were coming the other way. The flow of people, the spaces between them, the spots where you could just squeeze through if you wanted—you suddenly feel like you can see it all. You can feel yourself registering these details, even as you take care that nobody bumps into Female Warrior. So this is the difference between those who have ventured into the dungeon and those who haven't. Although you would do it again if given the choice once more, you now realize that you were truly risking your life when you took up that fight on behalf of Female Bishop.

"...Mm, I'm okay now," Female Warrior says, shifting and shaking her head as the tavern comes into view. You glance down at her, and she looks away, peering at the ground to conceal her face. You cock your head, puzzled; several adventurers pass you by, their gear clanging noisily.

When you suddenly connect the dots, you look to your party members, asking them what to do.

"Oh come on, who cares? What's the point of putting up a front now?" Half-Elf Scout says with a grin. "It don't get much more humiliating than bein' on the edge of death. What's wrong with a little embarrassment, am I right?"

"...Just you remember this...," Female Warrior mumbles, but even her veiled threat sounds weak. As you smile and start forward, another adventuring party passes by. They're awfully enthusiastic. It's all you can do to keep Female Warrior out of the way—although you don't begrudge them for a second.

Just as you all thought earlier, it really does seem like a festival around here. Adventurers and common folk alike choke the main thoroughfare, everyone looking unusually excited.

"It's sure nothing like it was this afternoon," your cousin whispers to you. You doubt it's like this every night, and yet...

The furor reaches its highest point as you push through the door of the tavern. You're assaulted by a wave of noise so loud, it makes your ears ring. It isn't directed at you and your party, of course, but nonetheless, it's overwhelming. Most perplexing of all is...

"Welcome, welcome!"

...the crowd of gorgeous waitresses who greet you with broad smiles when you enter.

"...Is something happening?" Female Bishop asks you, and you aren't quite sure how to explain it to her. Among the things she probably can't see are the rabbit ears bobbing atop each of the girls' heads. Also the fact that they're covered by only the barest excuse for clothing. They don't look like your average waitresses.

"...See no evil," Myrmidon Monk clacks quietly. "Not that I particularly mind."

"You kiddin'?" Half-Elf Scout asks, checking the girls out with affected cool, but he receives only a clack in return.

"Yeesh." Female Warrior groans to discover what uncouth men she's keeping for company. Then she says to Female Bishop, "Don't give it a second thought... Doubt it has anything to do with you yet anyway."

"Uh...huh. That's fine, I guess...," Female Bishop says, not sounding completely convinced.

You remain flummoxed as to what could possibly be the source of all this hubbub. You open your mouth to ask about it, but your *second* cousin silences you with an elbow jab. "Er, excuse me, may I?"

"Oh, yes, you have an order?" one of the rabbit-eared waitresses says, coming over.

Your cousin is thoroughly flustered seeing her clothes (or lack thereof) at close range, but, looking away and blushing, she says, "No, I… I was just wondering what's going on today, if anything happened. We just got back to town a few minutes ago."

"Ah!" the waitress says, nodding and smiling. "Well, a stairway down to the third level of the dungeon was discovered!"

You open your eyes in surprise—no, really. You're not staring at the woman's ample chest. Really.

For all the threat the spreading Death poses to the Four-Cornered World, the survey of the dungeon is not proceeding very quickly. You came to this town to try to rectify that situation, but it seems someone is a step ahead of you.

"That party over there," the waitress says, pointing. "They're really something." She indicates a round table at the center of all the excitement. There you can see adventurers who look like weathered warriors. One is a red-haired monk, another a padfoot warrior. There's a fighter in silver armor; a massive wizard; an old, sagely type; and a girl with silver hair, so small she almost doesn't seem to be there at all. And then you see the Knight of Diamonds sitting proudly among them, and you let out a breath. He's calmly sipping from a mug, his armor sparkling, no sign of fatigue on his face.

Compare that to your utter exhaustion, leaning on your friends just to stay on your feet, more eager to go to bed than to have a drink. The two of you couldn't be more different. You realize he's far more than one step ahead of you. You can practically picture him, beautifully engaging in combat two floors beneath the surface, discovering a rich hoard of treasure, and staying in the royal suite tonight. He's on another level, literally and figuratively, in comparison with you and your struggles with goblins and slimes on the first floor.

"…" Female Warrior takes in the Knight of Diamonds and his party, looking even more aggrieved than before. You let out the slightest breath. Gods—you couldn't be more different in every way.

"Hmm? Something the matter…?" Your cousin's voice surprises you, but you shake your head and insist that it's nothing. You realize you've been squeezing the scabbard of your sword, and you let it go with a sigh. Finally, you tell the waitress that you'd like somewhere to stay and ask if they have room in a stable.

§

Where do adventurers with no money stay the night? There's only one place: a stable, often available for free.

You request simple beds for the women, afraid of making things too hard on them, but as for the men, you suck it up and sleep on piles of straw. According to Myrmidon Monk: "Just spreading a cloak on the ground is plenty. For me, at least."

You and Half-Elf Scout follow his example, but you can't seem to get to sleep. It's not that the stink of the horses bothers you, and it isn't that the pile of straw is especially uncomfortable. You haven't lived such a pampered life that you've never had to deal with such things before. More likely, it has to do with the combination of exhaustion and anxiety, excitement and nerves. That's what you decide. No matter how desperately your body wants to sleep like a log, your mind is convinced it's still on the battlefield and won't allow it.

This is one more bit of proof of your inexperience. Just look at Myrmidon Monk and Half-Elf Scout. They're sleeping like babies. You gaze up at the ceiling of the drab stable, and finally you decide to get up off the straw pile. You hang your sword at your hip, then step outside, greeted by a breath of wind. It's the same night breeze you felt when you arrived back at the surface from the dungeon.

Squinting against the chilly wind, you notice a bright light shining in the dark night sky. Thinking it must be the moons or the stars, you look up to discover it's coming from the windows of the tavern-inn, and you can't suppress a smile.

You walk calmly around behind the building. You're not going anywhere in particular. Maybe you just wanted to see the light from the windows. Hey, the stars and the moons aren't the only things that can be beautiful.

If each and every one of the lights in those windows represents an adventurer's sleeping place, then it could be satisfying to gaze at them. As you walk, you think back on the Knight of Diamonds and his friends from a few minutes earlier. The memory mingles with thoughts of the battle you fought for your lives in the dungeon, one you're almost embarrassed to describe in such terms.

That's it: That's the gap.

The difference between your party, struggling against the most minor monsters, overjoyed by a single treasure chest—and adventurers on the front lines. What you feel isn't anger or regret; you don't even think of yourself as pathetic. You simply find yourself accepting the bare, unavoidable fact.

You take a breath of the cold air, then let it out. It helps cool the heat inside you.

You draw your sword, which catches the light from the windows. It helped carve the path of blood before you this day, and you check its condition carefully, making sure the fastenings are all secure. A katana is more than a simple weapon—that's what the person who taught you the sword said. It is a part of you, an extension of your body, your technique, your very spirit. So let all be as one. Join mind and body with the blade, fuse intention and action. For you, to think must be to act.

You have not, of course, achieved that ideal yet. The most you can do is to obey the teachings of your mentor and, at the very least, make sure your sword is in good shape.

Many are those who seek famous blades, renowned swords, weapons of legend, and you don't blame them. But your mass-produced katana is still nothing to sneeze at. For starters, this dully glimmering blade saved your life today.

"Hee-hee. And what might you be up to?"

You almost jump at the unexpected voice coming from just over your head. You look up, and there she is. Leaning out the window in nothing but a rough-hewn nightshirt, a woman is resting her cheek on her hand. In the faint light, you can tell it's Female Warrior.

"Oh, surely I don't surprise you that much anymore." She seems to be enjoying how startled you are; she narrows her eyes like she's smiling but presses her lips together as if in a pout.

If she's up there, then those must be the economy rooms. You slide your sword back into its scabbard with a *click*. You ask if she should be up and about yet, to which she replies, "I'm fine," with a giggle. "It was just a little suffocation. Not a flesh wound."

That's good to hear, but you hope she won't overdo it. You can't help noticing, meanwhile, how large the economy rooms appear to be. Are your cousin and Female Bishop in the same room with Female Warrior?

"They're both out cold. Maybe they were tired? They're sound asleep."

That *second* cousin of yours... When Female Warrior hears you grumble, she gives you that giggle again. In fact, something—you don't know what—must be really funny, because tears start to form at the corners of her eyes. She wipes them away with an "I'm sorry," then follows that up with a question. "Tell me—that girl, is she your older sister?"

You respond firmly that she isn't, that she is in fact your cousin, who just happened to be born a few days earlier than you.

"That right? You two just get along well, then."

Well, you won't deny it. She can be careless, but even in some other life circumstances, you don't think she would be a bad person.

"Better not stay up *too* late, or you'll be in for a scolding from your dear older sister."

'Speak for yourself.'

"Good point," Female Warrior replies with an earnest nod and then falls silent. You raise an eyebrow, offering to listen if there's something she wants to talk about. She doesn't respond immediately, though, and you add that if she doesn't want to talk about it, that's fine, too.

It's not that you aren't curious, but what matters is how she feels. You can't force her to say anything. Just when you're thinking you might as well go do some practice swings, though, Female Warrior says softly: "Tomorrow, I hope we'll all have plenty of time to get together and... Well, before that." The words are soft, slipping from between her lips like droplets of water pulling free. "I think I'd better apologize for today."

Now, what could she be talking about?

You feign ignorance, but she shakes her head and says, "Come on." She looks right at you. "I appreciate you and the girl trying to spare my feelings. But you're our leader, right?"

In other words, it's your job to oversee the party's fighting strength. And if there's any baggage, any ball and chain, then the smart move is to cut it loose. For everyone's sake. To adventure is to risk your life; every move, every step could save you or kill you.

'Ah,' you say, *'leaders really have it rough—a lot of responsibility.'* But Female Warrior blinks as if she's misunderstood you. She doesn't seem to grasp what you're saying, but you don't see the failures of earlier as such great crimes. Eventually, everyone encounters their crisis. Try as you might to avoid it, it's best to proceed on the assumption that it will come eventually and to be prepared for it. From that perspective, you simply extricated yourselves from a problem today. What's wrong with that?

Not to mention (you laugh), if you chased Female Warrior away because of that, then you *would* hear it from your cousin.

"I see..." Female Warrior looks mildly perplexed by your words but nonetheless nods. "That's good, then." What matters is the problem is resolved.

You nod, then casually take up a stance with your sword, raise it, and bring it down. There's a whoosh of air. Then you do it again, making sure your joints are warmed up and loose. Then you do it again and again, over and over until the heat in your body finally dissipates.

You hear Female Warrior exhale where she watches from above you. "I'm going to bed, then, okay? Don't burn the midnight oil too much longer—you really will get an earful."

You nod and say good night to her, that you'll see her tomorrow. She doesn't answer right away. Your sword goes up, then comes down.

After a moment, you hear the window close, along with a quiet: "Yeah... See you tomorrow." The words are soft, but you're sure you heard them.

See you tomorrow. A good expression. You have tomorrow. Tomorrow will come.

You're inexperienced, and your party members are untried in some ways. The dungeon is deep, the road ahead is long, and the monsters are fearsome. But there's always tomorrow.

You are alive, your party members are safe, and the dungeon can be faced.

There's always tomorrow.

With those thoughts in your mind and your heart, you raise your sword up, slicing through the air.

"Ugh! Stay *away* from me!" Female Warrior cries, looking on the verge of tears, as she shoves away another pile of goo. The slime, caught on her spear tip, slams into the wall, where it bursts with a wet *splat*.

How many does that make? you wonder as you watch Female Warrior flail away at the monsters like a child with a stick.

"I'm so sick of these things…!" She's already destroyed quite a number of them, spurred on by her personal hatred of slimes. You can't bring yourself to laugh at the sight of her covered in red that looks just like blood spatter, even though it isn't.

Your scout, who's been checking out the enemy composition, comes rushing back toward you. "Cap, there's more of 'em up ahead!" In the distance, down the wire-frame hallway, you see the hazy figure of some monster. The miasma in the dungeon makes it hard to tell exactly what monster it is.

"If you don't know what you're fighting, best assume it's a dragon."

According to your master's old advice, that thing could be far more threatening than some dead slimes.

Without a moment's hesitation, you bring your sword down on the skeleton-like silhouette. The instant you do, you hear a sound like shattering pottery, and the enemy figure flinches back. There's no spray of blood, but instead white shards graze your cheek before disappearing into the darkness behind you.

©lack

'An undead kobold!'

"Good, then it should be vulnerable to Dispel…!" Myrmidon Monk says, his mandibles clacking as he forms the sigil. In an instant, the oppressive, moldy smell of the dungeon is swept away by a breath of fresh air. That breeze is the blessing of the Trade God, who protects travelers, and it causes the skeleton soldier to clatter to the ground in pieces. Perhaps the creature was once a dog-man padfoot who wandered into the maze and never made it back out, or perhaps it was summoned by another Non-Prayer Character. In any event, even a padfoot would think it was the skeleton of a dog now, the remains of this monster that was half-dog and half-lizard.

Considering how desperate you are to conserve your spells, you're grateful this was all it took to bring the undead creature down. But then…

"It's still moving!" your cousin exclaims from behind you.

And indeed, although its movements are now clearly very awkward and stiff, the skeleton hasn't stopped. You quickly position your sword, low and to the left, then close the distance by sliding your feet across the floor. You don't have to be too frightened, you think, but at the same time, there's never any telling what will happen in this dungeon.

"No worries! This'll finish the job!" Half-Elf Scout comes rushing past you, slamming the hilt of his dagger into the skeleton and breaking it apart. Instantaneously, the creature collapses into pieces as if the string holding it together had snapped. The collection of old bones sinks into the sea of slime, a somewhat disturbing sight despite the lack of gore.

You've heard it said that the power of the Death down here, which is like a virus, sometimes causes even Turn Undead to be ineffective. This time, though, somewhat to your surprise, you seem to have managed it. Perhaps that's the small blessing of still being on the top floor of the dungeon.

"I'm sorry—perhaps I should have lent some aid…?" Female Bishop asks, calmly smashing one of the surviving slimes with the sword and scales. You look around cautiously, your sword still at the ready, but shake your head at her. You can't be afraid to go all out when the moment calls for it, but committing everything every time will only exhaust you. You feel that if this was enough to get you through safely, then that's all that was needed. Female Bishop smiles slightly when you say as much. "I'm glad, then... Er, a-also, could I have you check over the map?"

She sounds somewhat apologetic, having been right in the middle of the mapping when the fight broke out, but you don't mind. You expect enemies inside a chamber, but this was a random encounter. Sudden is sudden, no matter how prepared you might be. You wipe the filth from your blade and return it to its scabbard, then take the sheepskin paper Female Bishop holds reluctantly out to you.

This is excellent. You look at the map and grunt appreciatively. It isn't the most technically accomplished thing in the world, but it's very neat. Even considering how uniform the construction of the dungeon is, one similar segment after another, it's still impressive work for a woman who can hardly see. Most of the first floor is already accounted for, hallways described by charcoal lines and carefully notated.

"Man, wandering monsters never have treasure chests," Half-Elf Scout complains as he rifles through the monsters' meager possessions.

"It's all good. Experience is experience," Myrmidon Monk replies, still keeping watch vigilantly. Half-Elf Scout looks at him and shrugs.

Myrmidon Monk might have given Female Bishop some pointers, but she did the rest on her own. You tell her the map is well drawn and will serve nicely, and you see her face soften ever so slightly into a smile. "You...really mean that? I certainly appreciate it, but..."

None of you has anything to gain from lying. You pat Female Bishop on the shoulder in reassurance, then let out a sigh. You've been coming down into this dungeon for a while now, and it seems like things are proceeding apace for you. That's not to say you can afford to relax, but...

"It's true—we've started to get used to this work." Your cousin is grinning. You admonish her not to let her guard down, then turn to the last person in line.

"Urgh... Yeah, we're fine, but I'm sure never letting my guard down around a slime again..." Female Warrior is crouched on the ground, still mumbling about her hatred of these creatures. Her entire body is stained a light pink; you almost smile as you toss her a rag she can use to wipe off. "Thanks," she says weakly, blotting at her face and hair. She's messy but uninjured.

Slimes specialize in ambush attacks like hanging from the ceiling and then dropping on an enemy's face to suffocate them, but that isn't their only trick. Getting hit by one is a lot like being nailed by a full waterskin, and some of them can land pretty hard. Even if they aren't acidic or poisonous like the ones you've heard about in rumors, you know it's still bad news to fall victim to one of their surprise attacks.

You know that but...

After a moment, Female Warrior rises to her feet, saying, "...They didn't even touch me. Gosh, what is wrong with me...? I really have to get myself together." She grabs her spear and does indeed appear to have pushed away the worst of her thoughts. But even from your brief acquaintance, you know enough to suspect she isn't quite as calm and collected as she looks.

Slimes are either the best opponents for her or the worst... Every time you see her engage them, you're never sure what you should say to her. There's never been another call as close as that first trip into the dungeon, but every encounter with slimes leaves her dripping wet. Why? The way she presses the rag to her face afterward gives you an inkling. Maybe it's that, despite being in the front row, she spends an instant paralyzed by surprise whenever slimes appear...

"Mn... There. Yeah, phew. I'm all good now."

Well, in any case, it's not as if slimes are the only thing in this dungeon. You've never seen her fazed by any other foe, no matter how strong, and she always gives her all in every fight—so there's no problem.

"Oh, I'll get you a new rag later, okay?"

You don't particularly mind, but she's already squeezed out the sopping cloth and put it in her bag. You decide to accept her graciousness for what it is. You ignore your *second* cousin, who's looking at you and grinning for some reason, and heave a sigh. The battle is over. There are no more enemies. Your allies have sustained only minimal injuries and fatigue. No need to return to the surface yet. Having reached this conclusion, you turn to the two people at the very back of your party.

They're wearing crude equipment—although, to be fair, it's not so different from yours. Two young women. Their frightened faces make them look younger than they are, but you recall they're fifteen or so, making them of age. You ask if they're all right continuing the expedition, to which they nod back at you with exaggerated motions. "Y-yes, w-we're fine."

Good, then.

You aren't exactly the most experienced adventurers in the world yourselves, and you and your companions can't be constantly keeping an eye on these two younglings. All the more so during a fight—you're starting to appreciate what a good idea it was putting them well in the back.

The other problem is where the girls wanted to go... Are you really going to be all right on the way?

One of the girls says, "Um, there's a chamber just past here, and then..."

"Right," says the other. "You go through it, and there's another chamber... Everyone should be waiting in there, I think."

Even as you nod, you grumble to yourself.

The difference in strength between those who have gone into the dungeon even once and those who haven't is substantial. Even more so is the difference between those who have been down several times, like you, and those who have been here only once. You're not sure what to think of these two who pushed this far despite having been into the dungeon just one time—reckless, perhaps.

Despite your experience, though, you're hardly the most powerful things in this dungeon. You don't exactly have a lot of extra energy or resources to help someone out, but you offered it to them anyway. And what are you helping them with? Helping *their* friends!

You can really feel the weight of a burden you chose to accept, and almost without realizing it, you sigh again.

§

You think back: Maybe it all started around the table in the tavern that morning.

"I've been thinkin', and I think maybe it's best to let the captain handle money matters," Half-Elf Scout said, taking a couple of cards from his hand and looking for new ones.

"Well, I don't really care who does it. Last thing we want is to die in the dungeon because we were busy arguing over money." Myrmidon Monk took Half-Elf Scout's cards and dealt him a couple of new ones off the top of the deck, his mandibles clacking all the while.

Here in the fortress city, it was not particularly unusual to see adventurers playing cards in the tavern. The soft light of a morning turning into an afternoon streamed through the windows, warming the air inside the tavern.

Over days and days of your party resting between adventures, this particular round table had become your de facto reserved spot. The moment you entered the building, the rabbit-eared waitresses would smile at you and lead you over to it.

Or at least they would until you and your party died.

You don't exactly spend that long in the tavern at any given time, but you try to poke your head in when you have a break before and after an expedition. So this wasn't the first time you had seen such things. A party of adventurers who had been sitting around a table in the morning wouldn't come back that night. The table would still be empty the next morning, and the day after that, a different party with brand-new equipment would fill the seats.

That was just how life went here in the fortress city. No doubt someone else once sat at the table you now occupied. And no doubt someone else would sit at it after you were gone.

"How about you? What are you going to do?" The question brought you back from your reverie; you glanced down at the cards in your hand, then passed one to Myrmidon Monk. The man who suggested this round of the card game Fusion Blast dealt you another with the practiced air of a professional. You took it and, while trying to remain as expressionless as possible, asked if they really wanted you to handle all the money.

"Good question. As your older sister, I have to worry that you would blow it all on something silly." Your *second* cousin put her chin in her hands and looked melancholy. You glared at her as if to say, *Shut up.* What had she been thinking, agreeing so eagerly to this game of cards? Anyway, you don't think your *second* cousin is one to talk about the wise use of money.

"I guess it's all right," she said. "Managing money is a form of experience, too. Don't worry—your big sister will be in your corner!"

That annoyed you, but it seemed to mean she was in favor of your holding the purse strings.

At that moment, it was just the four of you sitting around the table piled high with breakfast and playing cards. You would have to ask Female Bishop and Female Warrior their thoughts when they showed up, but in any case, consolidating the group's resources definitely seemed like a good idea to you. Whether you were in charge of it or not, it was important that somebody had a grasp of the party's overall budget. After all, the quality of one member's gear didn't affect them alone. It could be a deciding factor for whether the entire party was more or less likely to survive. If the warrior in the front row couldn't afford to buy decent armor, it meant the life of the spell caster in the back row was in danger. As long as unequal spending didn't become a problem, there were many advantages to having a communal purse in a party.

"You, changing cards?"

"Hmm... I think I'll stand." Your cousin tilted her head slightly; you questioned whether she understood the rules or not.

"I like your confidence," Myrmidon Monk said, his compound eyes sparkling as he spread out his hand. "I've got Lightning."

You played a Magic Missile combo, while Half-Elf Scout clicked his tongue and played a pair of Sleep cards.

Now only your cousin was left. At your urging, and with some reluctance, she turned her cards over. "Um, I think these all go together. You think so?"

Fusion Blast.

Myrmidon Monk silently put down his cards and pushed the entire pile of dried grapes over to her.

"Hee-hee-hee, thank you very much!"

"Gah! Sis, I can't tell if you're a world-class gambler or just lucky as hell!" Half-Elf Scout said. Frankly, you weren't sure, either. In your experience, it was rare for her to pick things up quickly or thoroughly, but it never seemed to hurt her. In fact, as much as it killed you to think of her as an adventurer, she always seemed exceptionally lucky.

"H-hello… Sorry I'm late…" You heard footsteps pattering toward you despite the din of the tavern. Female Bishop was heading for your table, her hair disheveled and her face flushed. You'd learned from working with her that she seemed to prefer to wear her hair down. You pulled out a chair for her, and she almost fell into it, working a comb through her frazzled hair. "I went to the temple to offer my morning prayers, but it took longer than I expected…"

"Hee-hee, well, g'morning. Sometimes a little walk to the temple is just what the doctor ordered." Female Warrior ambled up from behind Female Bishop.

Now your party was complete. Female Warrior cast a critical glance at the battle raging on the tabletop, then grinned. "Not playing any dirty tricks, are you?"

"Sure ain't," Half-Elf Scout said with a sour look. "If I was, Sis there wouldn't be holding the whole damn pile!"

Female Warrior giggled and said something teasing about how silly he looked. Beside her, Female Bishop just seemed confused. Your cousin giggled at them and pushed her loot in their direction. "How about some dried grapes? I can't possibly eat all these myself."

You three men were still sleeping in the stables, while the girls shared the single large room upstairs with simple beds. It wasn't precisely *because* they were women, but you thought some courtesy was called for. You had no way of knowing, though, how the ladies spent their evenings up in the big room together.

The men and women of your group had one thing in common: They didn't all show up for breakfast at the same time just because they roomed together. It seemed like your cousin wanted to hurry up and eat this morning, so their group had split up and moved separately. On that note, you had a little trouble imagining Female Warrior being eager to go pray…

"Heh-heh, what is it?" She gave you an uncharacteristically cold smile, and you shook your head and said it was nothing. Maybe she was just being nice to Female Bishop. That made sense.

Anyway, it was more important to ask how they felt about the management of the party's finances. You brought it up after they had both ordered breakfast, and Female Bishop clapped her hands and looked at you. "U-um, I think it would be best for our leader to oversee everything." What could you say to such naive good faith?

"Ooh, I think she likes you," Female Warrior teased, leaning against your arm. "Me, I could use some new gear, you know…?"

Aw, get off. You shook her away, and she leaned back, giggling.

"Gosh!" your cousin scoffed, staring daggers at you. She seemed to be offended that you could take such an attitude toward a young woman, but if she wanted to be mad at someone, it should have been Female Warrior, not you. Stupid *second* cousin.

Myrmidon Monk, apparently wishing to change the subject before things descended into name-calling, clacked his mandibles and asked, "So what do we do today?"

Judging by Female Warrior's reaction, you didn't think she had any objections to your holding the purse. So obviously, the next thing you had to do as leader was to decide the party's business for the day.

"We have some money," Myrmidon Monk said. "So do we do a little shopping? Or do we head back down because we've had a rest? I don't care either way."

"He's right—we've got a nice little nest egg going. Might be time to start thinking about new equipment…" From his bag, Half-Elf Scout produced items you'd obtained on your last expedition and placed them on the table. Gold coins were easy enough, but when you got equipment from a treasure chest, you had to find out how much it was worth before you could do anything with it.

"Wouldn't expect much from a chest on the first floor," Myrmidon Monk said.

"True enough. Things might be different another level down…" Female Warrior nodded.

Whatever they wanted to say, enemies were the greatest limiting factor. You were just reaching a point where you could battle the creatures on the first floor more or less safely. In other words, you were finally a match for goblins and kobold skeletons. And from the least of the monsters in the dungeon naturally came the least of the treasures.

Then again, anywhere outside the fortress city, the contents of their coffers would have been considered quite a windfall…

"Them's the breaks, Cap. Slow and steady gets us to the lowest level!" Half-Elf Scout said, clenching his fist for emphasis. You agreed completely.

"All right, looks like it's your time to shine!" your cousin added with a nod at Female Bishop.

"Certainly," she answered. "If I may?" She closed her eyes and reached out to the various objects on the table. Her capacity to identify items, granted by the gods, was quite something. If you had no other way to figure out what something was, you could always ask a shop to identify it, but the service came with a steep price. Most adventurers weren't businesspeople, and their ability to discern the true value of a certain item was, generally speaking, not very good. There was always the possibility, too, that what seemed like a rusted or worn piece of junk at first glance might actually be a magical weapon. If you wanted to make the most of your adventures here in the fortress city, the ability to identify items was essential.

For a young party like yours to have someone like Female Bishop was heartening indeed. And with her ability to use magic and miracles, she proved a stalwart ally in the dungeon as well. This line of thought always left you wondering why so many other adventurers had discounted her as a mere item identifier, but putting that aside…

"That's just the way it is," Myrmidon Monk said, speaking softly in deference to the concentrating Female Bishop. "They were paying her. And the customer's always right, allegedly. It gives them a big head. Can happen to anyone.

"*Plus, there's the fact that she was defeated by goblins.*" These last words were little more than a whisper. *But*, you thought, *it happens*. No one wins every battle.

"Then there are the scruffy men you hear rumors of," Myrmidon Monk continued.

Scruffy? You cocked your head at the unfamiliar word.

"They're—y'know," Half-Elf Scout said, "adventurers. Sort of. But they became so obsessed with money that now they see even their colleagues as nothing but potential sources of coin."

"Are there really people like that?" your cousin asked, her eyes wide as if she couldn't believe what she was hearing. She wasn't accustomed to thinking of people as capable of such evil. You always thought that was one of her strengths.

As for you, though, it didn't seem too shocking. People weren't as special as they liked to think. Not the good ones and not the bad ones. Anyhow, shady work was an undeniable part of how the world worked. *The devil made me do it*—that's what people often said.

"Oh, yes there are," said Female Warrior, to your surprise, her voice quiet but unmistakable. "The scruffy men really do exist." She sounded like a child who had seen a ghost, who was insisting, fearful and sullen, that it hadn't only been her imagination even as the adults laughed over her. You nodded. If Female Warrior said they existed, then you were sure they did.

She didn't say anything more, though, and you simply waited for the identification to be done. When she was ready to talk, she would. This was no time to press her.

So when she turned a clearly forced smile on you, you didn't make a big deal about it. "Well, aren't we having fun? Like eager kids." Even if she was just trying to change the subject, she wasn't wrong—you *were* eager to find out what all this stuff was. It was your loot from the dungeon, after all. You were perfectly well aware that it wouldn't be anything too impressive, but that couldn't stop the twinge of excitement you felt. You had no complaints about your ordinary sword, but suppose you could lay your hands on one of the magical blades spoken of in legends… It was impossible to stay completely calm at the thought.

"Did we even find any swords last time we were down there?" your *second* cousin wondered with a puzzled look, but you shot back that there was nothing wrong with hoping. You had found some mysterious weapons, and dreaming a little was perfectly normal. That, at least, was free.

After a time, Female Bishop looked up, wiping the sweat from her brow and letting out a breath. "I'm finished. But…"

You leaned forward. *'Thanks. How was it?'* You were very curious. Katanas—were there any katanas?

"No, er… I'm afraid not. Some Rusty Chain Mail and Rotten Leather Armor…"

What a mess. Female Bishop looked on, a little lost, as you groaned and suggested the party sell everything—not much else to do. At least you would still get some income. Yes, that was what counted. Junk like this deserved to be sold.

"Don't suppose it would do us any good to haul it around. More to be gained by just selling it all off."

"Yeah, the man's right."

The other guys patted your shoulder consolingly, but you knew perfectly well that they were smiling. You gave them a glare, only to be greeted by chuckling from your cousin. "How about we take today off, then?" she said.

"Yay, shopping trip!" Female Warrior exclaimed with all the enthusiasm of a little girl. Whether she meant it or not was difficult to discern.

Still, it fell to you to make the final call. You could send everyone into town. Invite someone else along with you. Deliberately go out on your own.

What to do; what to do…

You were just about to open your mouth when a girl shouted, "P-please! Somebody help us!" Her cry could barely cut through the clamor of the tavern; it was swallowed up almost immediately. A few of the adventurers hanging out at the bar glanced toward the doorway, but nothing else happened. It wasn't out of a lack of humanity. More like a simple judgment that there was probably nothing to be gained by doing anything.

When you glanced over, you saw two young women, looking truly pitiful. One had her hair bundled cutely, while the other kept her long tresses neatly together. They were…not warriors, you suspected. They didn't look strong enough. But they were certainly adventurers. You wondered, back when you were a novice (not that you were all that experienced now), if you had looked much like them. They were dressed in the cheapest gear that could be found at market, their bodies soft and lacking in definition. They squeezed each other's hands, desperate not to let go, and they couldn't disguise their terrified trembling.

But what caught your attention was their eyes. The girls with their neatly coiffed hair were pushing aside their fear to peer desperately around the tavern. In spite of the long-haired girl saying, "I told you it was useless."

You let out a breath and looked around at your companions. Myrmidon Monk was the first to speak: "I don't care either way."

That settled it, then. With your other party members looking on grimly, you called out to the girls, asking what was the matter.

The face of the girl with her hair tied back lit up, while that of her companion went stiff.

"U-um, well, we, we need to rescue someone…"

Hrm. You put on a deeply thoughtful expression and stroked your chin pointedly. So this was about some friend who went into the dungeon and never came back?

"Oh, no, our friends are just fine…," the girl with the tail said, her voice going up an octave. "They just can't…quite move…"

"So we came here to…find some help…," the girl with the long hair continued, and you felt your eyes widen.

"Whoa, so the two of you got out of that dungeon by yourselves?! That's some trick!" Half-Elf Scout beckoned the girls over to your table, then called a waitress and ordered a couple of glasses of warm milk. Myrmidon Monk clacked his mandibles together in what sounded very much like a *tsk* but dutifully grabbed a couple of chairs from the next table all the same. The girls found themselves sandwiched between the two men.

"………" You let out another breath; from the corner of your eye, you could see Female Bishop looking at the floor so the girls wouldn't see her face.

"Maybe you could tell us what happened?" Leave it to your cousin to find a natural way to guide the conversation at a time like this.

The girls sipped at their milk, holding the mugs with both hands, clearly deeply relieved. Your cousin had scored a critical hit almost without realizing it. The two girls looked at each other, unsure who should talk, until finally one of them squeaked out, "Um, we were friends from the same orphanage, and, er...we decided to become adventurers."

"Oh-ho," Female Warrior said in a quiet, encouraging voice. The girls flinched, a little overwhelmed, but they managed to continue. In short, their story was this:

There had been six of them total. All women, all of whom had left the orphanage at fifteen years old and agreed to become adventurers. In this era when the Death held sway, they had scant prospects for the future, so they felt it best to make what fortune they could in the dungeon. Thankfully for them, their orphanage had been one of those associated with a temple, so they had some education and knew how to pray. They were better equipped (they concluded after considerable thought) than some youngsters who didn't know how to do anything except swing a stick. And so, several days later, they had arrived at last in the fortress city and joined the ranks of adventurers.

The rest hardly needed to be said. They had gotten their gear, made their first trip into the dungeon, fought a battle...

"And after defeating the monsters in that first room, we felt like we could keep going..." Even you noticed that Myrmidon Monk seemed to be uncommonly, and perhaps unintentionally, paying full attention to their story. "So we decided to keep going farther, but then..."

One of the party members had noticed it before the others: a dull thump that could be felt in their innards. The shock wave that came a moment later, nobody missed.

"Don't think there's anything on the first floor that uses magic like that— Musta been a bomb," Half-Elf Scout whispered.

"Yes," the girl with the tied-back hair replied with a nod. "So we thought maybe some other adventurers were in trouble..."

"Our older sister—the party leader—she said we should go take a look."

You muttered that all this seemed very unusual. Not just their party going to help someone they had never met but even the idea of encountering other adventurers in the maze. But you were sure they hadn't realized that. Not their first time in the dungeon.

You thought it must be the miasma in the labyrinth that addled the senses and prevented parties from meeting one another. It left adventurers without a great deal of interest in working with other groups—though luckily for these people, it wasn't impossible. You'd been down in the dungeon a number of times by this point, even if it was only to the first floor, and you had never once encountered another adventuring group.

"And then what happened?" your cousin asked, pushing the conversation along even as you sat lost in thought. Her calm tone of voice made the girls more relaxed as well.

"Well, we looked, you know, in some of the nearby rooms." Myrmidon Monk's face had gone grim again. "And then we found them."

"There... There were so many wounded people. Only one was okay..."

You suspected they had been injured in battle, near collapse, but were desperate not to go home empty-handed, so they had opened a treasure chest with too much haste. You thought back to your own first day. Female Warrior had been wounded on the way back, after you had already gotten your spoils, but if it had been during the fight in the chamber...

"We wondered what to do..."

The girls had been completely overwhelmed, confronted with the devastating scene before them. They couldn't simply abandon the dead. But there were also several seriously wounded present. They had been profoundly lucky to reach that room safely, but that day was their very first adventure. Even they understood that getting back to the surface with everyone in tow would be a tall order. And so...

"So she and I came here to find help..."

You involuntarily let out a sigh. Although you weren't sure if it was one of admiration or exasperation. To brave the underground world, just the two of them...!

"Ignorance really *is* bliss," Myrmidon Monk muttered. Was it reckless—rash—ridiculous? Whatever it was, you agreed with him.

But in any event, that was what had led to the sight currently in front of you. Two exhausted young women taking anxious sips of milk. Now that you'd heard their story, simply turning them down flat would be—well, not impossible. The reality was that their situation had nothing to do with you personally. And yet...

"..."

As you sat there thinking, someone tugged gently on your sleeve. You looked down to see Female Bishop, reaching out with a slim arm. To one side, your *second* cousin was practically champing at the bit to get going. As for Half-Elf Scout, he was grinning, while Myrmidon Monk shrugged as if to say, *Do whatever you want.*

"...You want to know what *I* think...?" Female Warrior said finally, and after a beat, she grinned. "I think the manly thing to do would be to help out a couple of damsels in distress, don't you?"

It sounded like it was settled.

You rose to your feet with a wry smile and hung your sword at your hip.

"Wha—?"

"Oh..."

The girls looked up at you in surprise. You scratched your cheek a bit awkwardly. You had been just about to decide whether you'd go into the dungeon today or not. What's more, you thought of yourself as a man who had more than self-interest at heart—and an adventurer to boot.

§

When you see everyone has collected themselves, you urge the group to continue. Everyone abandons their various forms of rest and relaxation inside the camp and gets to their feet. You call it *camp*, but it doesn't involve a tent like it would on the surface. Instead, you draw a circle with holy water from the temple, which you can rest safely within.

The effects won't last very long, but it keeps you safe from wandering monsters and gives you a chance to catch your breath. It's all too easy to lose your focus, so frequent rest breaks are crucial. However, sometimes, if you fall into a trap and immediately camp down as you try to ascertain the situation, you can end up falling into the same trap again. Perhaps it could be said that the real law of this dungeon is to always keep a cool head.

There's nothing at all to help tell the passage of time down in this shadowy labyrinth.

The faint white wire frame just visible through the dark is everything. There is no sound, no sense of other living beings; if you let your mind wander, you might suddenly feel as if the entire world has simply stopped.

The only things on which you can base any judgment are your party's vitality, their spirit, and your own hazy focus. You can sympathize with how it must feel for adventurers who have been done in by wandering monsters down here.

This world is a very simple place. Your level determines everything. The only rule is victory or death. It's certainly easy enough to be swept along by the atmosphere down here, an aura controlled by the Death.

"I can't believe you made it this far on your first adventure…"

You snap out of your reverie. Your cousin is talking to the two young women where they're crouched down, trying to comfort them. "But you need to be more careful next time!" Salient advice indeed. If it wasn't your *second* cousin giving it!

But then, it's helpful of your cousin to be looking after newer adventurers (what an odd thought) this way. You chuckle, down in your throat where no one will hear you, and then focus on how things are going with the rest of your party. You figure your cousin is still fine on spells, but you're not sure about everyone else.

"I've still got miracles. Stay or go, I'm good," Myrmidon Monk says flatly.

"I am much the same… I have some spells and miracles remaining as well," Female Bishop replies, nodding assiduously. "Oh, but…" She suddenly trails off. Maybe her vitality is low, or perhaps there's some other problem. When you ask, she looks at the ground in embarrassment. "I'm…er, I'm a little worried about the map."

"Very well. Give it here—let me have a look," Myrmidon Monk says, clacking his mandibles and reaching out; Female Bishop hesitantly hands the map to him. You aren't too worried; you know how neat her work is. But it seems she doesn't share your confidence. You don't exactly blame her. Confidence isn't actually that easy to come by. If having Myrmidon Monk check her work will make her feel better, that's perfectly fine.

"Hey, Captain, I think you're getting the hang of this leadership business," Half-Elf Scout says, pounding you on the shoulder with a grand gesture and interrupting your thoughts. What could he be talking about? You give him a pointed frown, and he wipes the smile off his face.

Of course, it doesn't feel bad to you. You grin yourself and take a look at your other companions. Female Bishop might be the only one who asked for confirmation, but the same idea applies to everyone: It never hurts to have someone else double-check your equipment and health. And often, that responsibility falls to the party leader—that is, you.

"Ahhh, I'm fine," Half-Elf Scout says, patting the knife at his belt. "I get to stay in the back row, and it's not like we've seen a bunch of treasure chests."

Even so, you know part of his attention has been directed behind him, where he dutifully keeps one eye on the new girls. Splitting your concentration that way can take a toll. Those who claim scouts and thieves are just walking lockpicks have no idea what they're talking about. It certainly isn't true of the one you work with, at least.

"Gotta say, though, I'm pretty surprised," Half-Elf Scout remarks, almost as an afterthought. You ask what about. "Aw, nothin'," he replies. "Just never imagined our lady over there would go along with a rescue mission."

"Oh yeah?" Female Warrior, suddenly the subject of conversation, smiles indulgently. "I just thought if I was the leader, I'd probably want to go rescue them... And how could I object anyway?"

"Sure, sure, that's fine," Half-Elf Scout responds, looking like he's not sure what else to say. Female Warrior doesn't stop smiling, but you get the distinct impression she doesn't intend to say anything more on the subject. She has the aura of a fighter who doesn't plan on letting the opponent too close. You look at her equipment, which still reeks faintly of slime. The battle earlier doesn't seem to have done too much damage, though.

"Man, if slimes had heads, I'd chop 'em right off—believe me!" Half-Elf Scout says.

"Hey. Watch it, now… Or do you *want* me to get angry?"

Half-Elf Scout sounded like he was only teasing, trying to mend the party's mood, but Female Warrior brandishes her spear at him. She looks very serious about it, which causes you to smirk and remark that it's all good, as long as things don't get out of hand.

Now then, you've taken care of the rest of your party, but you can't forget to do the same for yourself. You cinch down the fasteners of your armor, which you had come a little loose; drawing the sword at your hip; you check all the rivets. Finally, you use some spittle to polish the leather-wrapped hilt, making sure it's rubbed in well so it won't slip in your hand.

A chamber door stands before you.

According to the new girls, the people you're trying to rescue are waiting just ahead. But it would be a disaster if you had an accident now. You have to be careful. You call your cousin over, and she walks up to you with a bright smile. "Sure thing—just let your big sis handle it!"

Blasted *second* cousin.

Ignoring Female Warrior's smirk, you submit to your cousin as she checks your equipment. Her slim, pale fingers dance over connections and fastenings until she nods. "Yep, looks good. But I thought all the monsters in this room were supposed to be dead? It'll be fine, right?"

"No," Myrmidon Monk says, shaking his head. "We can't assume that."

Mm. You settle your grip on your katana, listening closely to Myrmidon Monk.

"Defeated monsters disappear for a while, but eventually they 'respawn.'"

That is the whole mechanism by which this dungeon and its endless supply of monsters—and treasure—works.

Monsters appear in these chambers, and treasure chests appear along with them. The phenomenon would be all the more unsettling, you think, if it turned out not to be man-made. That's what has you so convinced that the Death is likewise controlled by someone or something. Has no one else ever had the same thought? Or perhaps they have and have simply preferred to enjoy the endless supply of loot without thinking too hard about it. But at the same time, that's why it's such slow going working your way through the dungeon. At least, you think so.

"True enough. I'm all for being able to make tons of money, but this dungeon sure is a weird place." Half-Elf Scout lines up in the back row, holding his dagger in an ice-pick grip and rotating his arms to loosen them.

Beside him, Female Bishop is breathing deeply, trying to steel her heart so she'll be able to pray for spells and miracles. "I hope... I hope it's not goblins," she says, a tremble of anxiety in her voice.

You think goblins make certain things easier, and depending on their numbers, the *five* of you together should be able to deal with them. You tell her, then, that there's nothing to worry about, and she nods uncertainly.

"When he's right, he's right," your cousin says brightly. "We're all here for you, so everything will be fine!" She smiles. It's a talent of hers, this ability to sound so sure of something for which there is no evident proof.

You shake your head, somewhat annoyed, then glance at Female Warrior.

"Ready whenever you are," she says. Just that. She has her lance up, and her armor and equipment are set. You nod, then kick down the door with all your strength and rush into the room. The door collapses inward with a crash.

You charge into the darkness, where you discover a group of humanoid creatures.

The scruffy men!

§

You bat away the silver flash from the darkness, bringing your sword around in a great sideward sweep as you do so. You don't feel it strike anything. You didn't expect to, of course; you're just trying to keep the enemies at bay. There are five—no, six of them. And just three of you in the front to keep them in check.

You move forward quickly, gauging the distance carefully, taking up a spot where you can engage the two of them who have pushed through your ranks.

So they are *human.*

From up close, you can see it. Their clothes are dusty, their armor is just leather, and they carry daggers. At a glance, you could almost mistake them for adventurers, but eyes that sparkle with malice betray that impression.

"Wh-what should we do…?!" Female Bishop cries from behind you, distraught. You answer back: *'Anything.'*

These men took up arms against adventurers in the dungeon. They could hardly profess surprise if they got cut down.

"They're nothin' more than highwaymen…" Half-Elf Scout has already accepted what has to be done. You can tell he's used to this.

One of the men rushes at you while you're conversing; you catch his blade with the tip of your sword and flick it away. You need to draw the enemies to yourself. You slide closer, never letting your attention lapse, taking quick, shallow breaths.

They say that a human is at their most vulnerable when they've just exhaled. Before the movement, after. You have to read the breath.

'Could these really be the scruffy men we were told of?'

"I'm…not…*sure!*" Female Warrior sounds uncertain but punctuates her reply with a couple of stabs of her spear. In these dungeon chambers, the weapon's long reach is an advantage. Its sharp, thrusting tip can control a couple of squares, keeping the enemy from getting too close.

"I don't care what they are!" Myrmidon Monk raises his curved blade at an angle, holding it in a reverse grip as he prepares to parry. "If they're not undead, then we can kill them, so let's do it!"

You face the two creatures—you think of them that way even now that you know they're human—and wait for them to move, imagining yourself as a wall. Female Warrior is in her element, but direct combat isn't Myrmidon Monk's forte, and he won't be able to keep this up for long.

You want to take care of your opponents as quickly as possible and go support him, but this isn't exactly a walk in the park for you, either. The two scruffy men, one from the right and one from the left, come charging at you, matching their pace to each other. If you stop one of them, the other will get you; if you try to dodge them both, they'll have an opening that leads straight to your party's back row—that seems to be their plan.

There's no room for error.

You swing your sword with your left hand, stopping the attack from that side; with your right hand free, you grab the dagger at your belt and bring it up. There's a *shing!* as the hilt catches a blade. You push the dagger against the weight bearing down on it. Just in the nick of time, you feel a shock run through your right hand, the one holding the dagger, and there's a sound of metal on metal.

True, you had to improvise, but you still can't help wondering what your mentor would say if they saw this. It's an awfully poor excuse for a two-sword style.

Nonetheless, you smile as you drop your hips, pointing the blades at the enemies to either side of you. Few are those who would heedlessly rush in with a sharp weapon pointed directly at them. You quickly glance to one side, then the other, and start to close the distance with shuffling steps.

If they move, you'll exploit their moment of vulnerability to cut them down. If they don't move, you'll go on the attack at your leisure.

One of the men finally steels himself and flies at you, brandishing a dagger, and you meet him head-on. Right, left. Breathe in, breathe out. Let the sweat drip; just coordinate your blades with those attacks. At this moment, you are like a tree rooted to this spot. You just move your arms like branches tossed about by gusts of wind.

The law of averages is against your survival. If a third enemy was to join the fray, you'd be done for. And even as it is, you're not sure how long you can support the weight of your katana in a single hand.

But then again, you're not alone, either.

"I guess when you have to act...you have to act!" Female Bishop still doesn't sound quite sure.

"...Yeah, let's do it!" your cousin responds, seemingly talking as much to herself as to Female Bishop. "Sleep, together, in two moves!"

"Right!"

You can't be upset with the girls for coming late to the action. For one thing, you don't have any time to waste, but more to the point, you know how long it takes for spell casters to achieve the concentration they need.

One of the girls raises a short staff, the other the sword and scales, and together they intone words of true power.

"*Somnus!* Sleep."

"*Nebula!* Fog."

""*Oriens!* Arise."" The girls intone this last word together, the chamber ringing with the sound.

In an instant, an uncanny mist fills the darkness of the dungeon. Magic that addles the mind and brings on sleep is fearsome indeed, but how heartening to have it on your side. Before your eyes, the movements of your attackers grow slower, duller.

But even magic that can rewrite the very logic of the world is not all-powerful, not perfect.

"I'm sorry! I missed one!" A scruffy man slips past Myrmidon Monk and rushes for the back row. Maybe he was just lucky, or maybe he was especially alert; you don't know, but he was able to resist the magic.

"Like hell...!" Before the glittering dagger can reach the women, Half-Elf Scout throws himself in front of the scruffy man. He might not be able to defeat the enemy, but as long as he focuses on defense, he can buy you some time.

Your first priority needs to be closing ranks.

"...!" Female Bishop, though pale and biting her lip, brandishes her sword and scales and stands in front of your cousin. She's an adventurer and even has some training as a monk. She may not be very used to it, but she isn't completely unable to handle herself in hand-to-hand combat—whoever claims monks are useless is a fool.

"Hrm?" Somehow, the feeling of crisis makes Half-Elf Scout's voice sound louder than usual in your ears. He seems like he can hardly believe what he's seeing. "Heck, this guy's a rogue! And here I was all afraid he was a ninja!"

Does that mean they aren't very well trained?!

Your next actions are quick as lightning. You knock aside the hands of the man in front of you, already reeling drunkenly on his feet, and drive your dagger into his throat. You let go of your weapon and kick the body to the ground, then sweep around with your katana and cleave the other man's head from the chin upward. As you leap over the corpses and head for Myrmidon Monk's position, you call for help.

"I'm on it!" Female Warrior answers easily, running past you in the other direction.

You notice out of the corner of your eye that she's already taken care of her two scruffy men. Enemies who are barely awake are hardly opponents at all. No longer worried about the back row because you know you can leave it all to her, you grasp the hilt of your katana with both hands. Just ahead, you can see the back of the rogue Myrmidon Monk was fighting. You'll be there in two steps, one.

With a great shout, you slice through the gap in the side of his leather armor. The rogue howls and rounds on you, but it's too late. You raise your sword high, press forward, and deal a single terrible blow, cracking open his skull. A spray of blood and brains flies into the darkness of the maze, raining down around you.

"Thanks for the help. And...sorry. I screwed up there."

As you steady your breathing, still alert, you shake your head slowly. Stopping one of the two he had to deal with was a good start. Now, as for the back row— But at the same moment you turn around, there's an indistinct scream.

You wipe your katana and slide it back into its scabbard, then pull the dagger from the corpse's throat and do the same for it. The sound of it clicking into its sheath signals the end of the fight.

§

All right, is everyone okay?

You come down from the agitation of battle, trying to keep your cool as well as possible as you take stock. All you hear is the echoing of your party's ragged breathing in the gloom of the chamber. Blood and corpses spot the ground, but the six of you are still standing. Then there are the two girls you're escorting. Eight of you altogether. Your party, your "quest givers," and you are all safe.

"U-um, let me give you first aid..." You blink, surprised by Female Bishop's request. You don't seem to remember being wounded... "It's, um, your hand..."

That makes you realize that the tingle you felt in your right hand from that first move is still there. You look down to realize it was more than a tingle. The enemy's blade must have pierced through your glove at some point during the fight. There's a trickle of blood running down your hand. The moment you notice it, you feel a pain that pulses in time with your heartbeat, and you grimace.

The cut isn't deep and it certainly won't be a matter of life and death. You're sure your brain must have considered the pain irrelevant at the time. Still, it's a slipup not to have noticed sooner. If there had been poison on that knife, things could have been much worse. And poison or no poison, if you had been one beat later with your block, you could have been in real danger.

"Are you okay?" your cousin asks anxiously from behind Female Bishop. You assure them both that you're fine and remove your glove. The blood is welling up from a diagonal slash across the back of your hand; you press down on the wound. Stanching blood loss with pressure is the first step in any first aid.

"Well, that won't do. You've got to look after yourself, too, you know," Female Warrior teases with a snicker. But she's right. You nod. If you were to get caught by a slime or something, that would be *really* terrible.

"Erk…" She reddens at your comeback.

"Hey," your cousin says as if scolding a couple of bickering children. She jabs you in the side, albeit gently, and you ignore her.

Female Warrior looks like she's about to say something else, but Myrmidon Monk puts a hand on her shoulder. "We'd better find those girls' party. Unless you don't mind leaving them. I don't."

"Yeah, sure… I'll get you back later."

You find those words inordinately threatening. Meanwhile, you smile as you watch Myrmidon Monk and his bodyguard, Female Warrior, head off to search the chamber.

"I—I think it was you who was in the wrong, leader…" If even Female Bishop thinks so, then it's probably true. You'll just have to quietly accept your just desserts with good humor.

If nothing else, the bleeding seems to have stopped. A miracle won't be necessary in this case, but you would benefit from some medical attention.

"Don't worry—I'll take care of it," Female Bishop says, seemingly almost happy about your request; she produces bandages and ointments from her bag. "If you don't mind." She soaks your wound with a splash from her canteen and starts working on you.

With her fingers, she dabs some ointment from a jar onto your hand to prevent festering, then carefully wraps a bandage around it. She does excellent work despite her inability to see, and you realize it was the right choice to let her handle this. Now, as for the role of your beloved scout...

"Looks like they were doin' well for themselves, for a bunch of good-for-nothings." Half-Elf Scout comes back from rifling through the rogues' bags, looking very pleased. He tosses a leather pouch to you, and it jangles as you catch it in your left hand. You can feel coins inside.

"Better strip off their armor and equipment, too. Might get us a little something."

Half-Elf Scout gives you a toothy grin, and you nod at him. You accepted this rescue mission knowing there was no reward, but if you can make a bit of a profit along the way, so much the better. When you say so, Half-Elf Scout grins even wider. "Afraid there weren't any single-edged sabers like you're hoping for, Cap."

Bah. You're not upset, not really. But still—*bah.* You shake your head pointedly, but you hear giggling from a corner of the room. The two girls, who have been silent and grim until this moment, are suddenly smiling and laughing. When one of them meets your eye, she says, "S-sorry," and shrinks into herself, but you shake your head and say you don't mind.

The situation might be dire, but it won't be improved by moping about it. That's one of the things you like to think you've learned from your time in the dungeon.

"That's true," Female Bishop says. "B-besides, we won't know for sure until we identify everything, will we?" She's fighting to hide her own smile. As for your *second* cousin, she won't look at you, but her shoulders are quaking.

Sheesh. You let out a breath, thank Female Bishop for her help, and rise to your feet. You see Female Warrior coming back alone.

"We found 'em. Everyone is safe, I think. Girls, your party's all here."

The girl with the tied-back hair and the girl with the long hair look at each other, their faces flooded with relief. You respond with an acknowledgment, then check the condition of your sword and tell your companions it's time to move.

You know all too well what it means that Myrmidon Monk hasn't come back.

§

"O my god of the roaming wind, bear off the pain of these wounds, that we might resume our journey."

In the far corner of the chamber, you indeed find Myrmidon Monk invoking a Heal miracle. Inside a circle of holy water that appears to have been refreshed several times sit four young women looking petrified.

"Girls...!" The young women with you rush over, and when they're satisfied that their companions are all right, they allow their faces to blossom with joy. There are hugs and shouts, and as far as you can tell, the women are exhausted and frightened but not hurt.

"All's well that ends well," your cousin says, heading over to the girls. "Come on—you must be tired. Get a drink and a bite to eat, okay? I have some food here."

Damn, where was she hiding that?

Your cousin fishes her canteen out of her bag, along with various small baked goods.

"What? Treats can double as rations," she says with a giggle and a glance at you. Stupid *second* cousin.

But whatever—it's probably best to entrust the young ladies to your cousin's ministrations. For you, the more pertinent problem is the other party, the one that inspired these events.

"It's not good," Myrmidon Monk says quietly, looking up a moment later, his mandibles clacking.

"...No luck?" Half-Elf Scout asks, pulling one of the big hempen bags out of his pouch.

"Two," Myrmidon Monk says. "Another one's seriously wounded, but I've managed to stabilize them with first aid and miracles. They'll be all right if we can get them to the temple."

"Perhaps if I add my miracles...?" Female Bishop offers hesitantly, but you shake your head. You all still have to get home. Given the chance of bumping into wandering monsters, you'd like to hold something in reserve.

"Of course...," she says, nodding understanding. Then she adds in a whisper, "I hope it's not goblins..."

You say that personally, you'd like to avoid any slimes, too, and pat her on the shoulder.

"That's true..." The tension in her face relaxes.

Female Warrior puts a hand to her own cheek and exhales, defeated. "It's not like I'm afraid of slimes. Just don't like 'em... I mean that. Got it?"

You say that *of course* you believe her, then turn to the young women your cousin is tending to. The first person to stand as you approach has ringlets in her hair and looks to be the oldest of the girls; you assume she's the leader.

"I'm so sorry, making you go to all this trouble to rescue us..." She places a hand on her white leather armor that swells with a generous chest and bows her head with perfect poise and grace. For someone from a temple orphanage, she certainly knows her etiquette. Surely, you think, someone this refined would have had paths open to them in life besides adventuring, but you don't voice the thought. Every person has their own situation to deal with. You don't want to be nosy.

In a clipped tone, you tell the girls what you mean to do next, the pace of your speech indicating how important you think it is not to stay here for too long. You say that you're going to put the corpses in body bags, and the girls who are still living will unfortunately have to carry them. After all, you're looking at escorting an entire party of six girls, plus two corpses and four wounded. Twelve additional people altogether, plus their belongings: far more than your party alone can handle.

Not least because previous experiments with large groups in the dungeon have shown that one never knows when the miasma down here might suddenly separate some from the rest.

"Huh? You want us to what?!" One of the girls balks at your suggestion, but her leader quickly shoots a reproving "Come on!" at her. The girl bows and apologizes, but you give a shake of your head and tell her it's fine. They can leave the bodies here if they prefer. It's all the same to you.

"Hey!" Myrmidon Monk clacks an objection when he overhears you, but you smile and shrug.

"Grrr, how could you say something so awful to a bunch of young women?!" your *second* cousin exclaims from her corner of the room, and that shuts you up.

Bah, grrr.

Privately cursing your *second* cousin, you crouch down and start packing one of the corpses into a body bag. You might not be able to carry them, but getting them bagged up would certainly be easiest with more hands. When the girls see you, they quickly go to help another wounded adventurer.

These guys were lucky in their own way.

The corpses of most adventurers who die in the dungeon simply stay there, to be shortly forgotten and lost. Such corpses might become undead, wandering about the maze, or be eaten by monsters, or—it is said—made to serve other wicked needs of those who dwell down here...

Having one's body collected like this is chiefly the privilege of those who belong to large factions. Most adventurers can't hope for anyone to come and retrieve them.

"We'll have to be real careful heading back to the surface...," Female Warrior says while you work, and she keeps a vigilant watch.

You agree completely.

It's said that "the going is easy but the coming home a fright," and it's a given that you're going to be moving far slower than usual. Easy pickings for wandering monsters. Considering there are no guarantees of victory, the ideal would be to avoid any such encounters...

"Sure hope we don't run into any goblins..."

To your surprise, it's Female Warrior who says this. She's looking right at Female Bishop, who's crouched down, praying for the deceased adventurers. You voice your agreement as you cinch shut the body bags, now filled with their gruesome load. And not just goblins. You hope you don't run into any slimes, either.

"Are you ever going to let me live that down?" she responds, poking you in the leg with the butt of her spear. But there's a smile on her face.

You rub the armor over your leg, even though it didn't actually hurt, and start issuing orders.

"You got it, Cap," Half-Elf Scout says, jogging over. "But listen, we aren't planning to go busting into any rooms on the way home, do we?" He's grinning as he asks.

Well, unless some very unfortunate situation demands it, you don't have any intention or any spare energy to take detours. Half-Elf Scout nods when you explain this, then points at the hempen bags. "Then listen, with no chests to open, I don't have much to do. And I'd feel bad not making myself useful, so let me haul one of these guys around."

You smile wryly at his suggestion and nod. Half-Elf Scout happily tosses the body bag across his shoulders and exclaims, "All right!"

The leader of the young women, unsure whether to help or what to do, finally settles on a polite bow of her head. "Th-thank you…"

"Aw, it's nothin'. Adventurers help each other out, you know? I think I heard that from our captain once."

'Help and help alike.' With that brusque declaration, you set off walking, but you hear a snickering from behind you. You think your *second* cousin and Female Bishop are whispering about something. Bah.

Myrmidon Monk piles on: "…And how does *it's all the same to me* fit into that?"

"Yeah, just you remember that when we get topside," Female Warrior says, grinning like a cat. "Hey… You haven't forgotten already, have you?"

You remain resolutely silent, alertly scanning the path as you start back into the dungeon halls. From the chamber into the corridor and then the route to the surface. Back the same way you came. Should be fine.

"Ah, um, sir? I think we take a right next," Female Bishop says, running her fingers along the map. You nod and keep walking. Heading straight down the center of the wire-frame path, at this moment you feel as if you could take on any goblin or any slime.

What ultimately appears is a wandering skeleton—but it is no match for you and your companions.

§

"Ah, so it's them," the nun at the Trade God's temple says coldly when she sees the bodies you and the girls have brought back. She opened the door immediately when you knocked, even though it was the middle of the night, and was kind enough to take the remains from you. Considering her graciousness, you can't find it in you to get upset at her disinterested attitude.

The chapel looks pale and cold, illuminated by only a few candles and the light of the moons and stars filtering through the window. But even at this hour, you can see adventurers here and there in the stone room. People praying for either healing or repose for their comrades, you suppose. In other words, people like you aren't an uncommon sight around here.

An acolyte, still bearing traces of youth, kneels next to the wounded and begins ministering to them with a practiced air. The girls and their party watch anxiously, unable to settle down. The nun regards all this with a chilly eye, then offers a "Oh, very well. I recognize these people, and they've been fairly generous in their donations."

You flash a dry smile at this less-than-direct reference to money, but it also reminds you how powerful the stuff is. There are people here who will spare no effort to help you as long as you pay them—much more reliable than foolish, unrewarded devotion. Certainly better, at least, than the half-cocked rescue you and the girls pulled off.

"Think this means we'll get a material expression of gratitude?" Half-Elf Scout says teasingly.

"Pssh," your cousin admonishes him. "We didn't do this for money, all right?"

"Yeah, sure, I know. Just sayin'." Half-Elf Scout holds up his hands in surrender against your cousin's scolding. Female Warrior giggles, and your scout scratches his head in embarrassment. "Nothing wrong with bringing it up, at least. We came out okay, but it was a rough trip, right?"

"That's true. If anyone should get the gratitude, it's not us"—Female

Bishop's sightless eyes rove around the room—"but rather these girls, I think."

"Wha—?!" The leader of the young women, the girl with ringlets in her hair, jumps in surprise to find herself the subject of conversation. She waves her hand in front of her white-clad chest, as if waving away the idea. "N-no, we didn't do anything…!"

"Of course you did. We merely helped you." Female Bishop turns to you as if to say, *Isn't that right, leader?*

The girl with the ringlets looks from Female Bishop to you and back again, uncertain. You think for a moment, then announce:

'If you say you don't need any reward that might be forthcoming, we'll take it instead.'

You ignore Female Bishop's surprised "Huh?" and continue calmly that you incurred expenses just like the girls did. It would be too much to *expect* a reward, but you did as much work or more than the girls. So if they say they don't want whatever is offered, surely there's nothing wrong with your taking it.

Female Bishop is quietly objecting "Oh" and "But…" in the face of this supremely clear logic. Your *second* cousin looks like she wants to say something, too, but you ignore her.

What's more, you go on, the girls helped haul out the bodies, and there ought to be a reward for that.

"Oh…" The moment she hears this, Female Bishop's face blossoms like a flower, as if she realizes she's been laboring under a misunderstanding. "Y-yes, that's right. A reward! Yes, from us!" She reaches out, groping a bit until she finds the hands of the girl with the curly hair. "That would be all right, wouldn't it?"

"Er, y-yes—ahem. Y-yes, thank you. That… That might."

The girl nods unsteadily, to which Female Bishop replies with a joyful "Of course it would!"

"Ooh, Mr. Nice Guy," Female Warrior drawls, putting a teasing hand on your cheek. But you claim not to know what she's talking about. You make a show of checking the condition of the scabbard at your hip.

"I don't care either way," Myrmidon Monk says with a clack of his mandibles. His fingers quickly weave a sigil in the air, offering thanks toward the altar of the Trade God, and then he shrugs. "I just want to get home. Not interested in hanging around for something that doesn't pay."

But of course. You nod, then look at the nun, who has been watching you silently. Her eyes still look cold, yet then she smiles at you.

Even a pasted-on smile is still a smile.

"I like that attitude, everyone. I hope you'll keep it up."

You can't tell whether she's talking about the rescue or angling for a donation. But what's clear is that she's encouraging you. You smile back, bow slightly, and start heading out of the temple. Female Warrior follows you with light footsteps, and Female Bishop comes after her at a patter. Myrmidon Monk takes long, slow strides, while Half-Elf Scout looks relaxed but in fact moves quite precisely.

"Oh!" You hear your cousin exclaim before she scrambles after you. "Hey, that's not nice, just leaving your big sister behind like that!"

'Cousin, not sister.' You smile as you correct her, then reach out and push open the temple door. You're greeted by a cold breeze that caresses your cheek and then sweeps around behind you.

"U-um, excuse me!"

You turn, following the gust, to find the girls who asked for your help, led by the one with golden hair. They look nervous, working their fingers together uncertainly, but their words are clear and sure: "Th-thank you very much! W-we'll keep working and learning…!"

"Yeah, so… So let's adventure together again sometime!"

You laugh. Laugh and say, *'Of course,'* then resume your gentle pace.

Twin moons shine in the sky, and the lights of the town glow so that you could almost imagine you were in the middle of the starry sky.

"Man, our captain knows how to look good when it counts," Half-Elf Scout says with a grin, elbowing you gently in the ribs. You tell him to forget about it.

"I knew from the start he was a soft touch, but I'm beginning to think I joined the wrong party," Female Warrior adds.

"Don't I know it. No matter how old he gets, I can never take my eyes off him," your cousin says.

Let them talk. You pretend not to hear a word they're saying. Pfff. You can't trust a thing your *second* cousin says anyway. Yeesh. Seriously.

"Oh, I—I, er, think…it's a good thing…" Female Bishop smiles—awkwardly, yes, but she smiles all the same.

You purse your lips and say that yes, it's just fine, at which Myrmidon Monk clacks his mandibles especially loudly and says, "Pfah, it's all fine. As long as you don't screw up."

At last you retire to your inn, considering the day's unexpected adventure concluded. You know the pile of straw waiting for you in the stable isn't an especially distinguished place to sleep. But you have a feeling that tonight, at least, you might sleep pretty well.

Exhausted, you may drop into unconsciousness without so much as a dream… But you think that isn't such a bad thing in the end.

§

"Welcome, welcome!"

"Good morning!"

Even so, exhaustion can't be banished in a day. Especially not when you spent half of it sleeping on straw.

You lean against your round table, groaning to yourself, the tavern filled with the morning babble of adventurers. The waitresses' bright greetings fly this way and that overhead. You don't think this will ever get easier, no matter how much experience you accumulate or how much training you do. Your whole body feels creaky, slow, as if you have lead in your veins instead of blood. But your head is clear. That helps the commotion around you resolve into meaningful words.

"Hey, did you hear? They say an army of the Death appeared on the frontier."

"Ugh, so that's it for this country, eh?"

"Nah, just bad news for a village or two. Goblins and wargs, ghouls, centaurs, and some lizardman mercenaries—that's all there was."

"Huh, it's not even worth hunting down that army, then…"

"Yeah, nobody carries a treasure chest out in the field anyway. A waste of effort."

"All right, what say we check out a chamber or two down on the first floor today?"

The adventurers are laughing and chatting together, not so much as a hint of unease in their voices. You pluck off a piece of straw you discover stuck to your clothes.

Not like you have anything to say about any of it.

You're no different from them, as far as puttering around the first floor. Everyone has their own reason for being down there, whether out of a sense of crisis, or duty, or something else. They can do whatever they want, and so will you. No reason for you to start anything with them.

You suppress a sigh at this thought, letting your head loll from one side to the other on the table.

"Oh…"

Then you spot Female Bishop. Perhaps she was listening to the conversation, too; her face is composed but expressionless. It almost looks like she alone stands apart from the whole great crowd in this tavern. After a moment's thought, you say good morning to her in a completely normal tone.

"Oh, um," she says, fidgeting awkwardly, her mouth open as if she never expected this greeting. Then after a moment, she clears her throat with a delicate cough. "G-good morning, leader… That is you, isn't it?"

You nod and say that yes, it is, and at last she smiles with relief. She isn't completely blind, but it must not be easy for her to identify someone sitting silently at the table.

Female Bishop quickly sits down across from you but cocks her head, perplexed. "Where are the others?"

You left them in the stable. It didn't look like they cared to join you for breakfast. You declare flatly that men who oversleep are men who may be left to their own devices.

"O-oh, I see…" You chuckle quietly, and she asks, "Is everything all right?" You say there's no problem. You're rather more curious as to why Female Bishop has come to the tavern alone. "Oh, yes. Actually, there was a little something I wanted to ask about the map…" *So she came here early.* With a bit of a sheepish grin, she digs something out of her bag.

You change places to better look at the map. Female Bishop spreads the roll of sheepskin parchment neatly on the tabletop, and you review it from above.

"I think we've covered most of the first floor by now. But this one spot..." She runs her pale fingers across the lines of the map. *Zwip.* You watch her with fresh admiration. To be able to read what's on the page from just the feel of the paper and ink is quite a trick. Finally, her neatly trimmed nails arrive near the edge of the sheepskin, in territory unknown. "...What in the world do you suppose this is?"

The space she's pointing to is blank, untouched by any mapping. It's not because there's no way to get there. If you were to follow the twisting hallways, you could reach it if you wanted. The dungeon—or at least this first floor of it—appears to be a perfect square, so you don't believe this area is solid rock. But for some reason, you've never set foot there yet. And eavesdrop as you might on other adventurers' conversations, nobody seems to talk about this particular place.

Well, now... You scratch your chin, thinking. You already know where the stairway down to the second level is, and you have all the information you need. Whether you mean to make more money or continue your exploration, you have no special reason to head over to that blank space. And yet...

"It nags at you, doesn't it?"

Yes, yes it does.

Although your primary concern is the way of the sword, you are still an adventurer. And no true adventurer lacks a sense of curiosity.

Of course, curiosity has led many an adventurer to their doom. For those who run illegally through the shadows, you hear, untoward interest in their clients' backgrounds can cause them to disappear.

Ultimately, you could call this a part of your own training. A leader's job is to be fully cognizant of their party's current level, their teammates' abilities, and the prospective challenges of any place they're going to take them. So the wise thing to do would be to start by getting some information about this blank space, but...

"That place? That's a dark zone."

The answer comes almost as a gift from heaven. You look up from the map at the unexpected voice to find a handsome man with golden hair standing there. It's the young lord—the Knight of Diamonds you ran into right when you first got here.

"You can't even see the wire frame of the dungeon in there," he says, tapping the space on the map. "I hear no one's ever come back from that area." He shrugs. "There must be *something* there, but if you get the idea that you're the one who's going to figure it all out... Well, I'd call that egotism at best."

"I see...," Female Bishop responds, knitting her brow in a frown. "In other words, whatever it is, it would probably be a tall order for us." You nod as well. Then you congratulate the knight on his discovery of the third floor.

The Knight of Diamonds seems almost caught off guard by your words; his eyes widen a little, and he scratches his cheek self-consciously. "I won't say it was nothing, but... Well, the dice simply rolled in our favor." Coming from someone who stands on the literal front line of the dungeon, this could be taken as less modesty than provocation. What prevents it from feeling that way is the young man's well-known virtue.

Then the knight shifts in place, giving you both a deep, elegant bow of his head. "You were of great help to me and mine last night. I'm the one who should be thanking you from the bottom of my heart."

Well, now. You make a puzzled sound. True, you rescued some adventurers from the dungeon last night, but were they under this man's command? It would be unusual for such a group to have faced destruction on the very first floor. Above all, you don't remember seeing him yesterday. So what could he mean?

The Knight of Diamonds offers with some embarrassment, "Ah, no, they're a secondary unit—or perhaps I should say reserve forces. Vassals of mine, you see..." They actually went into the dungeon without so much as a scout—perhaps afraid of falling behind on the glory.

You watch him as he speaks, and you realize just how young he is. You find him considerably less intimidating than the first time you met. Maybe your experience in the dungeon is telling. In fact, he might even be younger than you. Just fifteen or sixteen, perhaps, only recently reaching adulthood—not so different from Female Bishop.

Speaking of whom, she offers a question at a rather unusual word. "Vassals, good sir...? I've heard the term, but..."

"Ah. Well... Even the third son of a poor noble family, it seems, must worry about servants and followers." In his evident embarrassment, he's saved from looking completely pathetic by the diamond armor that glitters on his body. It hardly looks to you like something a poor noble would wear, but, well, you and the nobility must have different ideas of what constitutes *"poor."* To them, it probably still means richer than anything you can imagine. Probably.

You don't particularly feel the need to pursue the issue further than that, and you ask instead why the knight is here.

"As I said, I wanted to thank you." He sounds like it should be the most obvious thing in the world. "Whatever you spent on that rescue mission, I'll reimburse you for it, and I'm prepared to add a little extra as a sign of gratitude."

You give a slow shake of your head. You practically feel giddy, in fact. You were merely subcontractors, so to speak; you have no right to any reward. If he wishes to pay anyone anything, it's that party of young women who are entitled to it. If they refuse it, you and your party will accept the money to compensate you for your trouble.

"...Mm, is that so? I'll do as you suggest, then," the Knight of Diamonds says with another dip of his head; Female Bishop nods as if all this is perfectly just. You try your best not to seem too aware of her as you say with as much conviction as possible that adventurers must help each other.

"I see," the Knight of Diamonds replies, nodding. "Fine words." He smiles. "But the fact remains that I *am* grateful to you. If you ever need anything, tell me. I will help you however I can." He gives you one more bow, then excuses himself and turns on his heel. The way his armor sparkles as he walks away makes you think that nobility, even in poverty, is something awfully impressive. You don't believe you could ever learn to carry yourself the way he does...

"Huh, putting on airs again?"

At least not while Female Warrior, who's finally appeared in the tavern, is standing there giggling to herself.

§

When you turn toward the giggle, you find all your companions already gathered.

Hrm. You turn your gaze to them, trying to pretend as if nothing significant has happened, giving them a look as if to say, *Yes, what?*

"We caught the part where you said we were—what was it? Subcontractors? And gave away our reward," Female Warrior says, putting on a teasing pout.

Your cousin raises a disapproving finger. "That won't do—you have to consult us first about these kinds of things." She wags the finger. Grrr. Stupid *second* cousin. You glare at her, but she's smiling for some reason. She seems to be under a kind of misapprehension, for you did indeed consult with them. Both her and *her.*

"Wait, what?!" Female Bishop is quite surprised to suddenly become the topic of conversation; you can see her eyes widen despite her bandage. "Um, well," she says as you press her for confirmation. "Well...yes. He did consult with me before deciding." She nods and even smiles.

Oh-ho. Now it's your eyes that grow a little wider. You hadn't expected her to back you up quite so assertively.

"Assertively, sir?"

W-well, yes. You nod pointedly, and she only smiles.

True, it's absolutely true. The two of you consulted together and decided what to do. No problem. Or there shouldn't be.

"Man, Cap, you know how to make an ally," Half-Elf Scout says with an exaggerated shake of his head. His tone is reproving, but he's grinning. Then he drops a creaking sack on the table, one veritably bursting at the seams. "Eh, not like we didn't make *any* money this time—so no problem as far as I'm concerned."

"All this is from yesterday...?" asks Female Bishop, her face shining as if she's thrilled to have this work to do.

"Sure is," the scout answers with a nod.

"May I examine it?" she asks and promptly takes the bag with a look of pleasure. After all, she's in her element now, with the keen perception she has been granted as an identifier.

She runs her fingers over the surface of the equipment, almost in a caress, and although it's no more and no less than what she's done before, your cousin says happily: "Heh-heh, you look a lot more into this than you did when we first met." She sounds proud, almost as if she was responsible for it. You nod. Though Female Bishop seems to have known a difficult life, she's a good young woman.

The party sits around her at the table, and you roll up the map so it won't get in the way of her work. You instruct her to let you know if there are any swords, at which Female Warrior puffs out her cheeks and grumbles, "Doubt it…"

Yes, but there's always a chance. Say it is one in ten thousand. That means one out of every ten thousand times, you'd get what you wanted—and who knows, that one time might be the very first. Consider that piece of equipment right there, the one that practically has a question mark floating over it. When properly identified, it might be a sword.

"Yeah, sure." Female Warrior shrugs, but you're not sure she's convinced.

"So? What are we doing today?" Myrmidon Monk asks clackingly once you're all seated and have ordered your food. "Rest? Adventure? I don't care either way."

What, indeed. You cross your arms and think. Luckily, your communal purse is full to overflowing, and you aren't worried about paying for your lodgings. The normal impulse would be not to slow down, but maybe that isn't the best idea when you all exerted yourselves so much just the day before. You didn't even expect to go out yesterday. So…

"I'd like to take a rest," Female Warrior says before you can speak, making a show of rubbing her shoulders and sighing. "I'm *awfully* tired…"

You can hardly blame her, seeing as how she was attacked by slimes and everything.

"Hmph, you *would* say that," she grumbles, turning a cold look on you.

She's right, though; it's a question of fatigue. You try to maintain your cool demeanor as you say so. Nobody goes down into the dungeon every single day. You should rest for today.

"Ooh, then I'm going to use today to study some spells!" your cousin says as soon as you suggest taking the day off.

Being gung ho is great and all, as long as it's not just talk. At that, your cousin puffs out her ample chest as if the response should be obvious. "We can't let those kids from yesterday show us up. Can we?"

"Oh, uh, a-are you talking to me?" Female Bishop looks up from where she was letting out a breath and wiping away some sweat after completing the identifications. By way of describing the results, she adds courteously to you, "No luck, I'm afraid." Apparently, her way of saying there are no swords. What a letdown! "But you're quite right. I'll have to work on my magic studies, too…"

"Then we can work on them together!" Your cousin grabs Female Bishop's hand even while the cleric is still shooting you concerned glances.

"Think I'll go drop in on a friend o' mine, then."

"Feh, day off, huh? …Well, only leaves me one choice. Guess I'll go see what's up at the arena…"

The other men summarily ignore you; in fact, Myrmidon Monk can hardly hide his excitement.

Pfah. Fine. *Fine.* In this situation, there's just one thing for you, the keeper of the party's purse, to do. You'll have to take the time to sell off the equipment you garnered from the dungeon yesterday—not that you especially regret it. But you'll be alone…all alone! You ignore your friends' amiable chat about how they're going to spend their day off and pick up the sack.

"Say…" You feel a tug on your sleeve. You stop cold and turn toward the honeyed voice to find Female Warrior smiling at you. She's pulling your arm toward that soft chest of hers, a flirtatious move she must have learned somewhere. It's almost enough to leave you wondering whether she's with Order or Chaos.

"I told you I'd pay you back, didn't I?"

So why is it that, confronted with her beaming smile, you feel like a rat cornered by a cat? Yes, you do remember her saying something of the sort yesterday, if only vaguely…

"I wouldn't mind a new set of armor… Hee-hee!"

It doesn't sound like you can refuse, any more than you can choose what to do with your day off.

§

There's only one thing people in the fortress city talk about: the dungeon. When they pass each other on the street, they talk about adventurers the way people in other cities talk about the weather. *Oh, there's a promising novice in town*, they say, or they discuss the current state of exploration or speculate as to who might be the one to delve all the way to the bottom and confront the Death.

The knight who wears the diamond armor comes up especially often in these conversations. After all, he's beautiful to look at, a handsome young lion. Of course young ladies would be intrigued by him.

"♪…" You walk along, letting the rumors fill your ears, while just ahead Female Warrior seems to be genuinely enjoying herself. Her hips draw little arcs as she walks, her heels clicking on the city streets. Other than the fact that she's carrying a sword at her hip—a modicum of necessary protection—she could almost pass as any ordinary girl simply out enjoying the town.

"What—? Trying to get a peek at my butt?" She turns to you, her hair rippling as she smiles like a cat and giggles. You still aren't sure whether the expression is sincere or not.

You shake your head and say no but also add that she looks like she's having fun.

"You're not wrong. I haven't had much time to just relax since I came to this town." And indeed, she sounds quite at leisure at this moment. The touch of affection in her voice makes you decide not to ask too many questions. Everyone has one or two things in their lives they would rather not talk about. You might say that as long as those things don't bear on your own survival, then they're none of your business. She can talk about them if and when she desires. You don't have to know every single thing about someone before you can work with them.

Anyway. As she leads you deeper into town, you reflect on how complicated the place is. You're not keen on just meandering around with no idea where you're going. Surely, she could at least tell you the place she has in mind.

"Hmm? Didn't I mention it earlier?" she says, giving you a puzzled look that makes her seem very young—and in fact, you realize, she is very young.

And no, she didn't tell you. You say as much flatly. You assumed, from what she said at the tavern, that she had an armor shop in mind, though.

"Yeah, a place I've been to a few times. It's got a good feel, this shop."

Oh-ho. Your face relaxes, almost a smile, and you put a hand on your scabbard. A shop with a "good feel" to it might have some genuine masterworks in stock.

"Maybe," she says when she sees the look on your face, although it's not clear if she means it.

Best to hurry, then. Get there quickly and grab some gear.

"Yeah, yeah. I'm pretty sure it was...this way, I think."

You can urge her forward as much as you want, but she's still the only one who knows where you're going. She trots along like a cat out for a walk, picking the route with the most sun. The fortress city might be as easy to get lost in as the dungeon itself, but there are still places that get light from the heavens.

You turn off the main road, then turn once or twice again and find yourself in a hidden corner of town.

Some children, obviously merchants' sons and daughters, sit in a circle beside the road, competing at a game of tossing pebbles into the circle. Goodwives nearby do laundry in big barrels, treading on the wash as they chat together. This town might run on the loot that comes out of the dungeon, it might seem the province of adventurers and merchants, but there is still a routine here.

The hubbub of the streets fades as Female Warrior and you work your way along the side alleys, until presently you arrive at a cul-de-sac.

"Ah, here it is." She smiles and points at the sign dangling above the door that clearly indicates an equipment shop. Creaking softly as it swings in the wind, the sign looks brand-new—but then, this whole city is quite recent. Or maybe it's just hitting a certain age—

"I'm heading in," Female Warrior says, interrupting your thoughts. She pushes open the door. "Wonder if the old man's here today..."

And then suddenly, she disappears. Astonished, you take a closer look at the door only to discover it leads directly to a steep, narrow staircase heading downward.

"Heh-heh, what did I tell you? Good atmosphere, right?" Female Warrior giggles from halfway down the stairs.

You nod, then all but throw yourself into the gloom. You're almost too solidly built to fit; getting down the stairs is a real challenge. As for Female Warrior, notwithstanding her generous endowment, she's a lithe woman. Maybe it's a biological difference between men and women or maybe a difference in level between the two of you. Or even just a question of being accustomed to it.

When you finally squeeze your way to the bottom of the stairs, you discover a smithy's shop, dim but for a glowing fire. It's a cramped space packed full of various kinds of gear, and you can hear a hammer pounding within. You can feel the heat of the fire on your skin.

"Hoh, it's you, little miss." The master of the place is bent over, deep in this room that feels like a chamber in the dungeon. He's an old man boasting a beard and muscles so abundant, you could almost take him for a dwarf. He gives an interested sniff, wrinkles his face at Female Warrior, then looks at you. "Got a man with you today? Always knew you were the hunting type."

"Sure do," Female Warrior says, putting her hands together in front of her chest. "I was thinking I might wheedle him into buying me some new armor."

"That right...? And?"

Well, now. It seems that last bit was directed at you.

"What's the story with you, boss? Just a walking wallet?"

For a second, you don't quite understand what he means, but these final words help you connect the dots. You're looking for a bladed weapon, a sword. Something thin, sharp, likely to bend before it breaks.

The old man sticks out one weathered hand without a word. He's saying, *Show it to me*, you surmise. You take the blade, scabbard and all, from your hip, ignoring Female Warrior's interjection of "Wow, so heavy" and passing it to the old man.

"Hrmph, eastern make, eh?" He can tell just by the feel of it in his hand. Next, he draws the blade with a metallic ring. The shimmering steel reflects the orange light of the fire as he runs a finger along it, then presses it silently to the side of his neck. "Undistinguished but a solid piece of work. Don't know who made it, but it ain't easy to take care of. I can hone it for you, at least."

Hmm. You stroke your chin, unsure what to say. Is he insulting you or praising you? If nothing else, you don't feel malice from his review, and what he says isn't wrong. You don't think you need to let it get to you.

While you're thinking, Female Warrior says smilingly to the old man, "So about this new armor... I was hoping for something that fits a little closer."

"Hrm?"

"And if it didn't make my shoulders so stiff, that would be nice. Mail could work, but even tied with a belt, it just pulls on the shoulders so hard..."

You keep their conversation in earshot as you cast a glance around the shop. The place seems to be stocked with every type of armor and weapon imaginable. Swords, spears, axes, sticks, staves. Helmets and shields, body armor and mantles, and even a few potions. Merchandise is stacked on shelves that stretch up to the ceiling.

You've never thought of yourself as a country bumpkin, but this is enough to make your head spin. There are cutting tools, of course, along with cleaving blades and swords that appear to be of immensely fine craftsmanship...

Hmm?

You get a funny feeling as you look around the shop. Most of the merchandise is brand-new, of course, or otherwise secondhand... But your eyes are drawn to something that appears new *even though it bears signs of use.*

"Novices don't always last very long," is all the old man offers when you remark on it. "In fact, lately, a lot of them have been dying. Lots of idiots out there. And simpleminded fools, too."

Is that so?

"The idiots, they die. And the fools who think, *I'm no idiot; I'm being nice and careful*, they die, too."

Ah. You shake your head as if to chase away the recognition that he could have been describing you not long ago. Sometimes a lone survivor would bring back their friends' equipment and sell it. Or another party might find the bodies and strip them. In any event, there's every chance that your sword, Female Warrior's spear, or the other equipment your party carries could have wound up lining these shelves—or might still yet. Everything depends on your level and the gods' dice.

You don't precisely sympathize with the lost, nor are you frightened by the idea; there's just a sort of cold emotionlessness inside you.

"Hello?" Your thoughts are interrupted, as so often, by Female Warrior, a smile in her voice. You glance at her and see she has a hand to her collar, clearly bored; her expression doesn't change as she says, "I'm going to have my measurements taken now…"

Hmm. You cock your head. If that's what she's going to do, she should do it. You have no problem with that.

"Exactly how long are you planning to stand there?"

Oops.

There are no curtains or coverings anywhere in the store. You hurriedly toss the purse to her, then work your way back into the cramped staircase. You hear her giggling behind you, followed by an almost erotic rustle of cloth.

It seems to follow you all the way to the surface.

§

From somewhere deep in the fortress city, you gaze up at the blue sky, divided into squares. The clouds and the sun are the same as they always are, yet from here, they seem immensely high up, far away. You stand to one side of the door so as not to be in the way of other customers—not that you think any will come by.

The wind brings a breath of air bearing that special clarity of a city before noon. That even this vast, complex place should have fresh air must be a blessing of the Trade God. The bustle of the streets several blocks away reaches your ears. You hear children shouting and women chattering, although by the time their voices reach you, you can no longer make out the words. The sunlight is warm and comfortable, and you feel as if you were floating in the sea.

It's almost impossible to believe the Death is lurking directly underfoot.

So long as you delve the dungeon—indeed, so long as you have anything to do with it—the Death will always be with you. It's impossible to forget that. But if you did, maybe you could melt away into the peace here. You could spend your life crawling around the first floor of the dungeon, never too far from the entrance, making your living on the deaths of monsters. So long as you have no objective besides making money, you have no prospects, either. It would simply be death piled upon death. Perhaps then, when your days are like cold ashes, you could claim to have nothing to do with the Death...

"Hullo, mister. That's the look of a man with nothing good on his mind if I ever saw it."

The cheerful voice catches you by surprise, and although you don't take up a fighting stance, you look to the side. The owner of the voice is beside and just below you. A diminutive figure in overclothes who doesn't quite come up to your shoulders.

You ask who they are, but you're not especially alarmed. They're just out of range of you. If they meant to steal from you, they wouldn't have said something first. And for the time being, they haven't done anything to warrant you wanting to kill them. But then...the first problem with that is that the sword you always wear at your hip isn't there now.

Would you be able to settle this problem with the dagger you normally carry for backup, if it came to that?

"Ooh, look who's Mr. Worried," the stranger says, apparently realizing that you're sizing them up. They have a bit of a lisp. They laugh gaily.

Well, now. You're puzzled; you don't recognize the voice. You slowly turn toward them. The stranger is indeed wearing some kind of overgarment—you think it's a woman, though. The gentle curves of her body are visible despite her clothes.

She has delicate limbs and a modest chest, but her body is firm, almost sculpted. There's no mistaking it. You see only a few strands

©lack

of golden hair peeking out from under her hood—that and a grinning smile.

"No need to try to glare me into submission. I'm just a fan."

You're not sure what this means, but at the very least, this person doesn't seem hostile. You ask her suspiciously about this "fan" business, trying to feel out what she really wants.

"Yep, a fan. Of adventurers, you see. I like to watch them, see what they do. And if I hear some news I think they might be interested in, I bring it to them."

Hmm. A fan of you and your party would be a bit surprising, but it seems this person is an adventurer herself. You don't precisely buy everything she's saying, but you're willing to listen.

"Let me tell you what's been bothering you, mister."

Her tell you? *That* bothers you, you inform her with a raised eyebrow.

"That right?" She laughs as though your suspicion means nothing to her, then says: "Newbie hunting."

The wind gusts at just that moment, *fwoosh.*

'Newbie hunting.'

You repeat the words out loud, not knowing exactly what they mean but feeling a chill just the same.

"That's right," she says. "You were attacked by those scruffy men down in the dungeon, weren't you?"

You nod. Strictly speaking, *you* attacked *them* and finished them off, but, well, details.

"And there's tell of people selling a bunch of *almost* brand-new equipment."

You nod again. You think of what you saw and heard in the shop downstairs just moments ago.

"There are people who hunt novice adventurers down in the dungeon, then strip off their equipment." You think you feel something like a flag going up in your mind as she speaks. "At the beginning, they did it at the tavern. Get the kids nice and drunk, everybody's happy, then they'd take 'em out back, and *bam.*" She makes a horrifically comical gesture, whipping one of her pale arms out from under her mantle. It's a theatrical move, certainly, but also a fairly effective representation of smashing someone's head in with a club.

Lots of adventurers come to the fortress city. A novice's life is cheap.

"Thing is, that's against the law. So they learned to do the deed down in the dungeon. Then maybe it's a monster's fault, right?"

She seems to be seeking agreement, but you don't respond. You do, however, mutter that it doesn't make sense. These people may think of themselves as the hunters, but eventually they'll become the hunted. That's how monsters work down in the dungeon. Or at least, that's what many adventurers believe. It might be dangerous, but they exist to be killed and deprived of their loot. Everyone knows that.

"Who's to say? Maybe it's not about profit or gain. Maybe they just enjoy the act. Maybe they're possessed."

'Possessed.' Once again you repeat: 'possessed.' But by what?

No, you don't have to ask. You already know. It has to be…

"The Death."

Even with the wind blowing, the words reach your ears clearly.

The Death.

You gaze up into the sky with its division into squares. Suddenly, it seems covered in the shadow of the Death that wells up out of the dungeon.

"I hear they have a hideout on the second floor of the dungeon. Watch out for yourself, eh, mister?" She cackles and waves a hand. Instead of answering, you grunt.

You're the leader of a party now. A group of companions set on reaching the source of the Death and destroying it. You can't let the prick of pride or a deluded little notion of justice draw you into unnecessary battles.

And yet… Newbie hunting.

The words seep into your heart, formless and creeping, inescapable. It's as if the great wave of the Death that emanates from the dungeon has suddenly and unexpectedly taken on concrete form. It seems to you that if you're going to reach the deepest depths of the dungeon, you won't be able to avoid it.

After a few minutes' thought, you slowly shake your head. This is for you to think about, but not for you to decide. You're a leader now. So instead of making a choice, you ask her: Why tell *you* this?

"You know, mister, the answer's obvious: There's no real reason!" She laughs uproariously, as if to say, *What an idiot you are!* "It's just how the dice roll of Fate and Chance turned out!" And then, before you can say another word, she dashes off.

You reach out, but all your hand grabs is empty air—she's already vanished down the next side alley. You look at your empty hand, then pull it back angrily. What was it you meant to do if you had caught hold of her? You don't know. This is completely unlike you. But still...

What to do now?

"Hey there, what's the matter?"

The next ambush comes, as ever, from right next to you. Female Warrior has pushed open the creaking door and is looking at you curiously.

You shake your head and tell her it's nothing; she emits a "hmm" and squeezes out of the stairwell. You see she's wrapped in metal scale armor that fits her as neatly as ordinary clothes. The hem goes to just above her knees, and a belt is tied around her waist. Maybe that's what makes the lines of her body so evident.

"Here, for you." Before you can comment on her new armor, she tosses something at you. You instinctively catch it to discover it's your purse and your sword, returned to its scabbard. You put the purse back in your pouch without checking the contents, then pull your sword just the slightest way out of its sheath. It catches the sunlight, a sharp, shining silver. You nod—*this is good work*—then click the sword back into place and hang it at your hip.

"...Mm, is that all?"

You say you don't want to plant seeds of mistrust in your team by counting the money. She just *hmms* again. She sounds uninterested, but you can't help feeling this is a thought-provoking reaction of its own. Anyway, if you start thinking that way, there'll be no end to it. If she has something to say, she'll say it.

"You know, it must be past noon already. I'm feeling a mite peckish..."

You consider for a second, then suggest that in that case, you should return to the tavern. There's something you want to ask the others, and it's a little late to be wandering around looking for someplace to eat with no particular place in mind. Then again, you're not sure if the others will be at the tavern for lunch, considering how excited they all were to have a day off.

"Heh-heh. That's fine, then." She walks off, and you follow after. You turn down an alleyway, then double back, taking a route completely different from the one you came by—and then you're back on the main street. But this was so much faster than the path you took on your way over. There are so many ways to get around here.

Just before you emerge onto the main thoroughfare, Female Warrior interjects softly, "Say..." She turns toward you, the sun, like the road, at her back, and she smiles. A ripple runs along her scale plates without so much as a sound, the brand-new metal catching the light and shining. "What do you think of my armor?"

You give some short response to this question, and she snickers.

But you, you have no idea what she herself thinks of it.

§

"See? I knew you needed to study more!"

That's what your *second* cousin, pointing her finger at you, says upon returning that evening, very much true to form. You swat the finger away wearily and look down at the book open on the round table. You don't know where she got it, but it appears to be a spell book.

It's so thick and heavy that it needs a reading stand; with its ancient-looking metal cover, it practically oozes history. You pick it up and feel how heavy it is; it's more suited to some library tower than this tavern.

Apparently, your cousin and Female Bishop, seated squarely beside her, have spent the entire day deep in study of this thing. You're pleased that the party's spell casters are devoted to improving themselves—but where in the world did they get this thing?

"A dark-elf tradesman got it for us. It will be helpful." Female Bishop, from her place at the table, is unusually garrulous. Or maybe it isn't that unusual. This is the true her—beaten and hidden it had been but is now coming to light.

"Heh-heh-heh, we can't let those girls outdo us!" The *"girls"* your cousin refers to must be the ones from the orphanage. You never thought of yourself as an especially experienced adventurer, but the presence of people less experienced than you seems to have been a useful goad. Even you feel like you can't rest on your laurels.

Not everyone in the fortress city agrees on this point, but most believe the Death has only one source. The Knight of Diamonds might find it before you, or perhaps those girls will overtake you from behind, but... In any event, only one party can solve the mystery and arrive at the root of the problem.

And it's always possible that you might expire, still lost in the dream. Even if you're down in the dungeon only for money—most adventurers are—you can still be swallowed up by the maze.

The Death.

The words are like a shadow that clings to you.

"He said it's a secret text from another country," your cousin says with a smile, apparently oblivious to how you're feeling; Female Bishop nods. "It's going to be very helpful."

When you look closely, you see there's a hint of color in her cheeks. Seems reading isn't the only thing your cousin's been doing at the bar.

Money. Yes. Need to think about money.

You give a gentle shake of your head in an effort to slough off the slight chill that's been hanging on you all afternoon. You control the party's collective finances, not the private money of its individual members. But still, two unworldly girls buying a mysterious book from a dark-elf trader? It seems a little fishy... Wondering aloud whether it really is some kind of secret heirloom text, you cast a doubtful eye on the book...

Aha.

Now you see why your *second* cousin would be so engrossed by it. You don't know whether you could necessarily use everything in it just now, but a quick skim of the pages reveals any number of useful spells. No harm in learning these. Whoever this merchant might or might not have been, his wares seem to be legitimate. Then again, when you think about it, your cousin had Female Bishop with her, who has the power of identification. Would have been hard to pull one over on them.

"Heh-heh, what do you think? Does your sister know how to do her shopping or what?"

You ignore your *second* cousin (who's currently puffing out her chest triumphantly) and close the spell book. It wouldn't be a bad idea to learn a few more spells yourself for your next dive into the dungeon. For now, you've got your hands full with your sword, literally; you still have trouble using magic intuitively in the heat of battle.

You're loath to give your cousin the satisfaction of admitting she's right, but you agree that maybe you should study a little bit. You have to drag the words out of your own mouth, but you manage to ask the girls if you might be able to borrow this book sometime.

"Er, I...I think it's quite all right. I don't mind."

"Sure, of course! Don't worry—your big sis will keep a good, close eye on you until you learn everything!"

That would be your *second* cousin. You make a gesture indicating this conversation is over, then let out a breath. You have to get some funds from the party purse to cover your cousin's expenses.

Half-Elf Scout watches your (in your case unwelcome) bit of banter with your cousin and laughs. "I gotta hand it to you. My head hurts just lookin' at this thing."

He had said he was going to go visit an acquaintance, and ended up coming back around evening. You smile and agree with him. Well, of course it's difficult. The old tongue, the words of true power, used in casting magical spells isn't anything like the everyday languages people speak now. Not to mention the descriptions of the spells are difficult; sometimes you feel the best you can hope for is to understand what little you can.

Half-Elf Scout listens to your explanation and nods enthusiastically. "I can understand it if I want to; I can. But I can't just take a look and go, *Aw, yeah, that makes sense.* I ain't one of those types. Gotta say, though, Cap, I wouldn't mind learning to use a spell or two myself, y'know? Don't have the brains for it, though." Then he laughs. You give a dry smile yourself.

Knowing the words isn't enough to use a magic spell. You need intelligence and perceptiveness. It's a bit like it is for clerics, who can read scripture all day long and still their prayers might not reach the gods.

You ignore Female Bishop, who continues to nod and say that "it will be helpful," and look at Myrmidon Monk instead.

"Seems fine either way…," he says to your fishing for agreement, sounding even less interested than usual as he sinks into his chair. "At least when compared with thinking you've won, only to go buy a snack and find out you've lost."

You see. That's true. You nod—you absolutely couldn't care less—and pour some wine from the jar into his cup. Myrmidon Monk takes the cup, gulps down the wine with a clack of his mandibles, then shakes his head, his antennae bobbing from side to side. "…My deity loves gambling, so why can't I get a blessing over here?"

Fate, you suppose, is the answer. You give a noncommittal response and pour some wine into your own cup. Or perhaps it's Chance. When it comes to the roll of the dice, even the gods…

"Hey…" You feel a tug on your sleeve, almost a sort of ambush; the hand was just there so suddenly. "Didn't you say there was something you wanted to ask everyone?" It's Female Warrior, who until a moment ago had been showing off her new armor to everyone, now that they're all finally back. She must have finally gotten enough admiration to satisfy her, because now she's sipping a cup of wine. She looks at you with her most ambiguous smile.

You give it a moment's thought, then decide to say it.

Apparently, there are "newbie hunters" in the dungeon.

Half-Elf Scout is the first to react. "Wha—? You talking about the scruffy men?"

You nod and say probably—the scruffy men, who supposedly have a base of operations on the second floor. Those rogues you dealt with last time out, hadn't you all stumbled upon them right as they were busy trying to strip some novices of their armor?

"Now I get it," Half-Elf Scout says, crossing his arms and making a face. He sits back in his chair.

Your cousin leans across the table, her eyes a little wider than usual. "Now you get what?"

"When I was out with my friend today, Sis," the scout says, "we were walkin' around town, but the whole place felt…funny."

'Funny?' You cock your head, and he replies, "Yeah," his face very serious. "Like there aren't enough mid-levelers, like the new kids aren't coming back up… The dungeon, I thought it was just that way."

That makes sense. Many adventurers give up truly delving the dungeon, resigning themselves to making some money—but still. If there seems to be a great gap in experience, newbie hunters would explain it. Of course, plenty of people meet their doom by the monsters, traps, and simple confusion generated by the Death in the dungeon. Whether anyone is engaging in newbie hunting or not, the Death will continue to flow out of the labyrinth in all likelihood.

"Where'd you get this info exactly, Cap?"

Well…

Where *did* you hear it? You shake your head: You can't seem to remember exactly.

It was in the afternoon… No, this afternoon you talked to the old man at the equipment shop and Female Warrior—and no one else, right? Well, maybe you picked it out in the snippets of passing conversation at the tavern… It doesn't really matter how you heard it anyway. Very few of the rumors swirling around the dungeon are totally trustworthy. Instead of asking each other pointless questions, it would be much better to go find the truth with your own eyes.

There's just one question: Do you need to find the truth? Whatever happened to the adventurers who went into the dungeon, it was on them. Whatever happened to those girls from the orphanage or any other adventurers, it has nothing to do with you. And conversely, whatever happens to you has nothing to do with any of them.

You are the leader of a party, and the fate of your party members rests, to a greater or lesser extent, on your shoulders. You don't have one single, solitary reason to put your companions in danger for the sake of some other adventurers. You can go out of your way to confront these newbie hunters or avoid them entirely.

We're free to make either choice.

"…………"

To your surprise, as you're deep in thought, it's your cousin who leans toward you, her face serious. What could she want? You open your mouth to ask her, but—

"C'mon, you!"

Eeyowch.

You can almost hear the sound as she pokes you in the forehead.

"A leader's not supposed to make a face like that. You're supposed to talk—to your big sis and everyone else."

Even as you rub your stinging head, you try to maintain your composure as you look back at your cousin. That's all well and good, but surely, she doesn't need to attack you for it?

"But you weren't even looking around you. I think a little poke in the head is the perfect antidote."

Around.

That causes you to take a proper look around the table. Half-Elf Scout guffaws and pounds himself on the chest. "What'sa matter, Captain? Something on your mind? You just tell your old scout, eh?"

"Let me guess—you're in love?" Next is Female Warrior, grinning. "Well, sorry to rain on your parade, but I'm afraid the answer is no." She puts her hands together in front of her ample chest apologetically.

You scratch your cheek with embarrassment (even though you haven't said anything yet), and Female Bishop opens her mouth hesitantly. "Um, uh…" Although she acts unsure, you can detect her gaze from underneath her bandage; she turns to you and nods firmly. "If you're willing to talk to me, I'm certainly willing to listen… Okay?"

"Me, I don't care either way," Myrmidon Monk says, mandibles clacking as he offers Female Bishop a drink of water. "Whatever's on your mind, just spit it out."

Well, sheesh.

"See?" Your cousin grins, and you realize she never meant any harm. Seeing now that you're surrounded by the kind of friends who are hard to come by, you shore up your resolve and share your thoughts.

'I want to hunt down those scruffy men.'

You won't pretend you're doing it for the greater good, for the world or anyone in it, or even because you personally don't like them. You won't spout any nonsense about virtue, or evil, or being unable to forgive them for their crimes. It literally has nothing to do with you. No one's asked you to fight them, and you have no reason to.

Except you came to the fortress city relying on your own blade. Can those who would challenge the Death live with themselves if they run from some ruffians on just the second floor?

Yes, there's a proverb that says the wise man doesn't face a stampeding stallion but takes a road that avoids it. But you don't wish to avoid this first intimation of the Death in the dungeon. Instead, you feel strongly that you should cut it down if you can and move forward.

"..."

"..."

Your friends, after hearing your thoughts, look at one another in silent consideration. You're thankful for this. You feel immense gratitude that they give it genuine thought, rather than unthinkingly saying *That's right* or *I agree*.

Ultimately, the first to speak is Half-Elf Scout. "It's a tough one, but... If we're talkin' purely about whether it benefits us or not, gotta say the answer is a resoundin' no."

Female Bishop turns a bit red at that; putting a hand to her cheek, she tries to offer her own ideas in a hesitant voice. "Wha—? But... Is that really true?"

"Sure it is," Half-Elf Scout replies with a nod. He isn't explicitly for or against the idea yet, just stating facts.

"He's right *if* we limit the discussion to ourselves," Myrmidon Monk says. "This bunch is after freshly minted prey. Adventurers who can handle the second floor themselves would be too risky."

Meaning, you suppose, that if you simply continue getting more powerful and delving deeper into the dungeon, there's minimal chance that you'll be targeted by these people. That's the conclusion you draw about your current situation based on what these two have said. If you go on with your original plan to head down to the second floor, you won't be attacked by the newbie hunters. Not even scorched by the sparks from their activities. No need at all to go jumping into the flames yourselves.

"Still... Hmm. I think there's more to say. What about you?" Myrmidon Monk pulls your thoughts back to the argument at hand.

"Who, me?" Half-Elf Scout makes a strained face. "Eh, it means no newbies coming up the ranks. Life'd be that much harder when you're trying to bring up a new kid…"

Now, that, you understand. They're talking about what happens when someone in this place dies and is lost. Spending inordinate amounts of time teaching and training new people would slow down the exploration of the dungeon; it would, in effect, be a retreat from the front lines.

You can't imagine how deep the dungeon might be beyond that second floor. Still less whether the people now delving will be the ones to reach the bottom…

"But we can't just do nothing."

Of course your cousin would say that. She's such a good-hearted soul, much more so (you know all too well!) than you are.

"We can't just sacrifice other people when we know what's happening…"

"I agree that, er…um…it would be helpful," Female Bishop says, much as you expected. She still sounds a little hesitant and uncertain; maybe the drink hasn't quite worn off yet. But she tilts her head in an enticing fashion, a bewitching expression on her face, and says coolly, "Besides, they aren't goblins, are they?"

At the very least, you don't think they are.

That simple confirmation from you brings a "Right" and a happy nod from her. Her voice still carries a hint of ineffable fear, but now she's against the scruffy men.

Always expected those two girls to agree anyway.

"Can't say I'm a big fan," Half-Elf Scout remarks, his cup in his hand and a sour look on his face, and that's also just as you knew it would be. "Long-term thinking's one thing, but the short-term matters, too."

"But dungeon crawling was always going to be dangerous. It's only a matter of whether we confront it now or put it off until later," Myrmidon Monk counters, his mandibles clacking. "In this case, we happen to have avoided the danger. The next time, we might not be able to. Do we leave ourselves a little slack or gain some experience?"

You think you understand where he's coming from.

'Meaning?'

"I don't care either way."

You take in these varying opinions into consideration and nod deeply.

Myrmidon Monk isn't specifically for or against. That makes it two against two. Not that it's precisely your intention to decide things by majority vote, but if it was, then…

"………"

Female Warrior has kept her silence. She's just sitting there at the edge of the table. You'll have to ask, find out what she thinks about all this. Notwithstanding her occasional serious looks, she tends to poke fun at any real arguments.

You ask the question, and at the bottom of her voice, sounding almost confused, she says, "What, me…? I… I…" You nod, encouraging her to continue, and finally, in the softest of tones, she says, "…I want to…do something to help, I guess…" Her words sound uncommonly delicate and vulnerable. She pulls her feet up onto her chair and nods to herself like a little child. "I want to do something. This… It's about more than just us."

Fair enough.

Now you've at least heard everyone's thoughts on the issue. You nod again to show that you're thinking seriously. That makes Female Warrior giggle and smile just like she always does. "…Hey, if our leader says no, then there's no arguing."

"True that!" agrees Half-Elf Scout, and you smile in spite of yourself. "We're the ones who picked you for this job, Cap, so just make the call."

Myrmidon Monk doesn't say anything, and neither does Female Bishop, although she smiles ambiguously and rocks back and forth a little.

"See?" Your cousin looks at you as if to say, *Just like your big sis told you, right?* Bah.

But you have indeed found yourself with rare traveling companions. You can certainly go confront those scruffy men on the second floor of the dungeon with them or ignore the whole thing. The right to choose is in your hands. This is true freedom.

You announce your decision.

'Let's do it.'

To turn a blind eye to evil is to do evil yourself—isn't that what they say? Besides, you're going to fight the Death at the bottom of the dungeon someday. What are a few ruffians to you?

Half-Elf Scout and Myrmidon Monk nod.

"Oh, it's on!"

"So it would seem."

Now that you've made the choice, all that's left is to act. You were already planning to head for the second floor on your next visit to the dungeon, so nothing new on that front. There shouldn't be any problems on the way, assuming Female Bishop is good and sober by then. The real key is going to be how many resources you can conserve during the trip, knowing you have a big fight awaiting you…

"Mn… Thanks," Female Warrior whispers, but you shake your head and say that you didn't do anything to warrant gratitude. You just made the best choice for your party's future.

"Heh-heh." Your cousin scoffs. "Your big sister is happy to see what a sweet person her little brother's turned into."

'Hush up, second cousin.'

Then you raise your voice even louder and call for a waitress. You're going into the dungeon tomorrow. A little more to drink first won't matter. The laughter of your companions as they watch you call for more alcohol is lost in the hum of the tavern.

"Say, Cap, I heard that Knight of Diamonds is heading to the second floor tomorrow, too."

Oh-ho. You listen closely, although you don't stop drinking liberally from your cup. This isn't the first rumor Half-Elf Scout has reported this evening—he seems to come by a lot of them.

"That's because I'm a scout and a thief. Keeping my ears open is my job." He crosses his arms as if this was obvious. "Heck, if I didn't work on gathering information, I'd have nothing to do but open treasure chests."

You don't think that's all he would have to do, and you tell him so. He's helped you out in any number of different ways.

"Gotta be diligent—that's the real trick to staying alive." He grins and shrugs.

Makes sense—by his logic, he's been keeping you all alive.

"Yeah. That's why you just have to do your best opening those treasure chests," says Female Warrior, who's been listening to you, cheerfully stirring the pot. You can see that her cheeks are flushed and her eyes relaxed; you're not sure how many cups of wine she's had. "But if you're not sure about one, you have to let us know, all right? There are lots of replacements."

"Like me," Myrmidon Monk adds, his mandibles clacking. "My Precog miracle lets me foresee any traps that might be set on a treasure chest."

"Geez…" Half-Elf Scout wrinkles his brow to much laughter (and eating and drinking) from the rest of you.

Well, only as much eating and drinking as the last few little coins in this purse.

Each of you has had a good day off, raised your level, and now you pray for success in tomorrow's dungeon dive. Chances to raise a glass and revel with your companions like this are precious. The next time one comes, you might not be celebrating with the same people.

In this town where ash and death attend you at all times, just living is hard enough. That's why the adventurers you see always celebrate as they do. And you intend to learn from their example.

§

Regardless, the last thing you want is to die because of a hangover. You dump Half-Elf Scout and Myrmidon Monk, both brought low by their cups, into the haystacks, then head outside the stable by yourself. You can see one lone white trail stretching through the bright array of the heavens far above: smoke from the distant mountain where a dragon is said to dwell.

You remove the mass-produced sword at your hip, scabbard and all, and sit down beside the stables. The cool night breeze of early summer feels pleasant against your cheeks, flush with spirits. You draw your sword and hold it up, almost as if to shield yourself from the starlight. You check the blade carefully, make sure all the fasteners are fastened, and see that the sharkskin wrapping around the hilt is still a good fit.

Your mentor taught you that your sword is much more than just a weapon. It is an extension of your body, your skills, and your heart: It is a part of you. And whatever it may or may not be, tomorrow you will entrust your life to it. Maintenance is crucial, lest poor fettle cost you everything in the dungeon.

"Hmm… Funny place to sleep." The unexpected voice causes you to jerk your head up; you tighten your grip on the hilt of your sword, then relax it again.

"Ha! Yeah, I'm here." Female Warrior stands in the starlight, grinning like a little girl. She sits herself down in a pile of straw beside the stable, ignoring your surprise. The place doesn't have the typical musk of animals—maybe because it seems more adventurers than horses sleep here. Female Warrior presses her hand into the straw with an interested "Huh! Softer than I expected. Wouldn't mind curling up right here."

Not quite grasping what she really means—but with you, what else is new?—you change positions so you're facing her. Female Warrior moves as well, shifting her soft, supple body so it presses right up against yours. "Hee-hee, getting your hopes up? Sorry to disappoint." She giggles, but you just smile wryly and shake your head. "Hmm," she says disinterestedly.

But won't your cousin and Female Bishop be concerned to find her missing from their room?

"Let's just say the dear things don't hold their alcohol very well."

Out cold, huh?

You suspect it's almost certainly your *second* cousin's fault, but it's also understandable, considering they seemed to have been drinking since noon.

"Just when I was really feeling bored, I looked out the window, and I could see the stables. I thought I'd stop by to kill some time."

Ah. You nod in response.

Trying to be mindful of your snoozing companions and the other adventurers nearby, you begin attending to your katana by the light of the moons. But if anything, that seems to draw her interest further. Well, it's not like you're sleepy yourself yet. You wouldn't be averse to chatting for a while…

"…Heh, who am I kidding? That's all just an excuse."

You look up from your work in surprise and find yourself gazing into Female Warrior's eyes, which are clear and true. You wonder if she's ever looked at you so unflinchingly before.

"…Hey, thanks for earlier, y'know?" she says and smiles gently. Not her usual smile, meant to obscure her true feelings, but one that makes her look as young and girlish as she is. There's the hem of her clothing, then her pale legs, her smile, the warmth of her beside you, the softness of her flesh. You force yourself to glance away from all this, up to the sky. There you see the twin moons and the gentle wisp of smoke.

Her opinion mattered to you, of course, but it wasn't the decisive factor. It had been your suggestion to begin with, but the feelings of each individual weren't the only things that went into the choice. It was really a question of what would be the most beneficial for the party in the future. So it's nothing she needs to be so concerned about. And if anything happens because of it, the responsibility will rest with the one who made the decision: with you, the party's leader.

Over the course of several minutes, you explain all this to her.

"Hmm… That's real cool and all," she says quietly, looking at you critically. "I always knew you liked putting on a show."

With utmost seriousness, you object that it isn't "a show"; it's simply how you really are, and she just giggles and then falls silent. The only sounds that remain are the gentle rasp of breathing and the wind. You hear, too, the distant burble of the town and the tavern, but that's all.

With Female Warrior quiet, you replace your katana in its scabbard with a click, then loll onto the hay, lying and looking at the stars. There's a faint rustle of clothing. You can feel, somehow, that Female Warrior is looking at you.

After a moment, you hear her snicker again. "…Hey. Be honest: You were *sort of* hoping, right?"

'Hoping for what?' You laugh, then close your eyes.

Tomorrow will come soon. Scruffy men or no, it will be your first time challenging that second floor of the dungeon. The great and august leader of the party mustn't be short on sleep.

"True," Female Warrior agrees, and you can feel her stand up. Then you hear her pat herself down and some straw scattering around. "But maybe that was just a little hope there?"

This time you don't say anything at all, and she likewise goes back to the inn without another word.

So the night ends.

§

"U-urgh… My *head*… It huuurts…"

Morning comes to the fortress city.

You sigh at your *second* cousin as she goes wobbling down the main street. You know the bustle of the city's residents will soon carry away the chilly white mist and the morning silence. The town, just waking up, looks almost empty, yet there's an irrepressible feeling of life. Maybe this is the only town where that feeling might be disturbed by a group of adventurers clanking down the street in full equipment.

Why did she drink until she felt that way anyway?

"W-we have antidotes and stuff…"

She thinks you're going to use one of your party's precious antidotes on a hangover?

Your cousin looks so despondent that you elect not to say anything else. When you think about it, you realize this girl didn't have a lot of opportunities to go out drinking with her friends and companions back when she was living at home. There's no special reason to needle her about her failure to consider the consequences.

"Are you quite all right…?"

"Yeah, I… I'm fine."

From that perspective, it's rather surprising that Female Bishop, seemingly so obviously a daughter of a cultured upbringing, is apparently unaffected. She holds the sword and scales as she walks and even has the wherewithal to offer a kind word to your cousin. Well, everyone has their own past.

"Heh-heh, guess I should've asked for more medicine while I was at the temple," Female Warrior says with her usual inscrutable smile. You see this as rather a different matter from your lengthy chat with her and settle on a simple nod. It's clear that she, too, has no intention of bringing up last night.

You remain somewhat mystified by why she feels the need to put in an appearance at the temple so regularly, considering she doesn't strike you as especially devout. At the same time, though, it's not for you to question what your party members do. This is well and good.

"My friend was tellin' me that if you fall asleep drunk, you might sleep, but your spirit doesn't get any rest," Half-Elf Scout says seriously from beside you. He seems to have done his fair share of drinking yesterday as well. But elves and rheas aren't built the same way humans are.

"Doesn't matter one way or the other to me—just do us a favor and don't flub your spells," chides Myrmidon Monk, who you know for a fact has been chewing some herbs that are supposed to chase away hangovers. You silently hold out your hand, and with a "tsk," he produces a plug of the herbs from his pouch and gives it to you. Still without a word, you pass it back to your cousin. She blinks at it, then grabs it with both hands and stuffs it into her mouth.

"…It's so bitter!"

'Yeah, it's a hangover cure.'

That's all the response you have to her concern as you cut through the city and head for the edge of town. To challenge the pit, its fangs bared like a cruel animal, while suffering from a hangover would be beyond foolish. The opponent you're facing is the Death. Something or someone stretching out its hand from deep within all over the Four-Cornered World. Whatever it is, you'll never be able to handle it just puttering around on the first floor, but today is different. Today, you're going down to the second level. It sounds like such a small change, but you have to make sure everything is just right.

That's what you're trying to keep in mind as you pass through the great gate and head for the dungeon entrance. The royal knight standing guard already knows you by sight, but then, there must be many she knows. And perhaps just as many who die before she gets to know their faces—yes, those who succumb to the Death.

The sense of death intensifies as you get closer; to you, it smells like rust…

Female Bishop is the first to say anything: "I smell blood…" Her voice is so soft and detached, you almost don't realize it's her at first.

The knight guard stares at you curiously when you all stop just in front of the dungeon entrance. She looks like she's about to ask if you've caught a case of cold feet, and you wave your hand to dismiss the notion. If you were really frightened, then you would have to humbly accept the reputation as a coward that would pursue you. But if not, then it would be a dishonor to be thought one. And dishonor is a failure and would ultimately mean you would have to kill yourself to make it right, and you'd like to avoid that.

Still, to discover the dungeon so full of blood and death that you can detect it all the way on the surface…

"Sorry, make way! Coming through!"

By the time the voice reaches you, even you can smell the blood. Racing out of the dungeon, equipment rattling, comes a party you recognize. It's the Knight of Diamonds and a red-haired adventurer, supported by their party members. All of them are wounded, their armor dirty, and several of them are carrying companions slumped over their shoulders.

The Knight of Diamonds, in the lead, is just as bloodless and pale as the others, and he's hardly uninjured. For one thing, he has a rag soaked a dark reddish-black pressed against the neck of his armor.

Now, that's *failure.*

They don't have to tell you to get out of the way; they nod in acknowledgment as you step aside, then run past you without breaking their pace. As they pass by, your eyes meet those of the Knight of Diamonds, who opens his mouth as if he might say something to you. But the words take on no sound, and before you can tell what he was about to say, they're gone.

Your party, left standing there, takes a look around, your eyes finally settling on the guard. The knight guard shrugs uncomfortably but says nothing.

"Do you think it was goblins…?"

"I'm betting it wasn't slimes—that's for sure."

Female Bishop and Female Warrior both have trouble hiding the nervousness in their voices. You say very seriously that it could well have been goblins or even slimes. "Grrr," your cousin growls from behind you, jabbing you in the back, but you can't be bothered to notice her.

"Y'know… I heard their party was going to be hitting the second floor today," Half-Elf Scout remarks, and you nod agreement. Probably best to assume they were fighting the notorious scruffy men. Apparently, they're more powerful opponents than you gave them credit for. You must be vigilant, but this might also be your best chance. After all, the scruffy men have certainly been weakened by the fight as well. Now might be the perfect moment to finish them off.

"But that…," your cousin says to this, clearly concerned. "That makes it sound like this is no different from a monster hunt…"

Myrmidon Monk's mandibles clack, and for once he laughs. "It just means those bastards are Non-Prayers now."

§

To make a long story short, slimes certainly do show up, as do goblins.

"…!" Female Bishop's teeth chatter, her face pale.

"Argh, I can't take it anymore…!" Beside her, Female Warrior is wiping goo off her clothes, looking like she might cry at any moment.

Down amid the white wire frame of the dungeon, even the simple path to the stairway is not guaranteed to be safe. You can stay out of every room, yet you never know when you might run into a wandering monster.

You kick the gooey, spreading puddle—whether it's blood or brains or what, you don't know—and turn around. You ask if everyone's okay. The two girls in the back aside, it would be trouble if anyone was hurt.

"…A good scare fixed me right up!" your *second* cousin replies brightly, probably referring to her hangover. You think maybe it had more to do with the herbs you gave her, but in any event, you flick the blood off your sword and put it back in its scabbard.

"This place has one rotten Dungeon Master." Half-Elf Scout snorts as he frisks the corpse of a goblin lying in a puddle of foul liquid. "We fight, we risk our lives just like we do in any of the chambers, but *these* guys don't carry treasure chests."

"Guess they don't want people who are only after money going any deeper." Myrmidon Monk, like you, wipes his blade and puts it away. "You're right; the danger's the same, so let the coin-addled stay up here instead of being tempted to explore farther—that's probably the logic."

You get out your canteen and take a swig, then speak to Female Bishop and Female Warrior.

"Yes… I'm all right," Female Bishop answers with an uneasy nod.

"Urgh, my brand-new armor…," Female Warrior moans, pouting.

You're not sure whether these responses represent their true feelings or are just a front, but if they can pretend to be all right, then that's probably good enough for now. You give out orders, then start walking through the halls of the wire frame that leads deeper into the dungeon. You've managed to make it to right near the staircase without using up any of your spells, which seems like a good sign. You leave it to your scout to check out what's ahead, then ask about the path to follow.

"Oh, yes," Female Bishop says, quickly opening the map she'd rolled up when the battle started.

Your cousin peeks in from beside her, brushing the surface of the sheepskin with the same fingers that clutch her short staff. "This is about where we are, right?"

"Yes, I think that's where the battle started, so…to the east one square, then north…"

Fighting within a room is one thing, but this is the danger of a battle out in the halls. After all, you don't stand in one place while you're fighting. You close distance, open it up again, get pushed back, or fight your way forward. In other words, your position changes, and if you resume exploring without taking that into account, it's all too easy to get lost. If you were to step on a turntable and get spun around completely—you haven't encountered that yet yourself—it would be no laughing matter.

More than anything, getting too involved in some other task can cost you your concentration.

You try to steady your breath, made ragged by combat, and wait for Female Bishop to finish the mapping.

"There it is—we're taking the long way around the dark zone, and we should reach the staircase before long."

You nod acknowledgment, then give Female Warrior a gentle pat on the shoulder. Her sopping clothes stick to her skin, but you make it a point to act like you don't notice. "Hmph," she utters, whether she notices this or not, then follows you at a brisk trot.

You finally arrive at something that isn't so much a staircase as a sort of rope ladder. It hangs clear through a hole in the floor so that you can climb up and down. You wonder if it was left there by the first adventurers to brave this dungeon to its bottom or if it's been there all along. You don't even know if anyone else has ever really reached the lowest floor.

You go right up to the edge of the hole and peer down.

Darkness.

A square patch of black yawns in the floor. The harder you look at it, the more you feel like it's looking back at you.

"Wouldn't want to fall down *that*," Half-Elf Scout says with a glance at the hole.

"Maybe, maybe not," Myrmidon Monk clacks. "This dungeon does funny things to your senses. What's close seems far away, and what's well in the distance looks like it's just out of reach."

Myrmidon eyes are different from those of humans. Maybe the world they see is different, too. But regardless, what he says is right. The only visible things in this dungeon are the darkness and the faint white wire frame of the walls. Perhaps the invisible floor beneath your feet is really just that thin.

"So if someone was to go *Boo!* from behind you..."

You give your *second* cousin a cold stare.

"What, you think I would actually do it? Not me."

Good, then.

"Wonder who—or what—is waiting for us on the second floor," Female Warrior whispers, and you, taking her cue, say it's probably monsters.

"Monsters." It's a broad grouping, but there it is. Be they goblins or be they slimes, the monsters, in their wanderings, made this dungeon their home, so perhaps it was true what Myrmidon Monk said before. You were going to have to fight fearsome Non-Prayer Characters.

'Let's go with the usual arrangement.'

You and Female Warrior, along with Myrmidon Monk, in the front row. Female Bishop and your cousin, along with Half-Elf Scout, in the back.

That means it will be up to you to descend the ladder first and make sure it's safe for everyone else to come down. You grab the ladder even as you make the suggestion and are greeted with nods from the others.

"Might be best for me t'go down last, then. Gotta make sure it stays safe up here, too." Half-Elf Scout smacks his chest assuredly.

"If you don't mind, we would most appreciate that," Female Bishop says with a dip of her head.

With the front row heading down first, you have to make sure you'll be able to return in a hurry if anything happens. You transfer your sword to your back so it won't get in your way as you climb.

"Just to be clear, there won't be any *looking up* by the people who go down first, will there?" says Female Warrior, ready as always with an ambush. She brings her arms together in front of her voluptuous bosom and looks at you as if to say, *Will there?*

"Not interested." Maybe Myrmidon Monk thinks he's helping, but he does it with his characteristic bluntness.

Whatever.

"Now, now, be a good boy," your *second* cousin teases, evidently intent on twisting the knife, and even Female Bishop examines you studiously. Her eyes might not carry the light of vision in them, but her gaze can still be cold and sharp when she wants it to.

Fine, fine. You give a wry smile, then get a better grip on the ladder and give it a good tug to make sure it's firmly in place. Satisfied that it's not going to come loose too easily, you lower yourself into the hole, hanging in space. You let out a breath, feeling the rungs of the ladder against your fingertips. Then you begin a slow, careful climb downward.

Your companions vanish from sight above you, and then you're swallowed up by darkness. You're frightened, yes—but no one has ever attained victory by worrying. The best thing you can do is banter with your friends a bit to keep things lighthearted as you go. Being unable to do that, here alone in the dark, is perhaps the worst part of this. But you steel yourself and proceed down, rung by rung, toward a second floor you can't yet see.

§

In terms of what you see, the second floor is no different from the first.

The wire-frame maze floating up out of the darkness. The chill, unfeeling atmosphere.

You stand in the very center of the hallway, call up to your companions above you, and give the ladder a shake.

The first to follow you is Myrmidon Monk, who comes sliding smoothly down. You remark that he seems used to this, to which he replies simply, "Well, you know." You don't know whether it's some trait of Myrmidons or past experience, but in any event, you find it reassuring.

"Hold on a second, 'kay?" Female Warrior seems to be having some trouble; whether it's from the height of the ladder or from awkwardly trying to hold her spear, you're not sure. She spends a moment attempting to figure out how to avoid both dropping her weapon and getting entangled in the rope ladder, but in the end, she seems to give it up. She ties some rope around herself, diagonally across her chest, securing the spear on her back before finally making it down the ladder.

"Sorry. Waiting long?" she asks, landing lightly on her feet, as if she and her armor weigh nothing at all. You nod your admiration. Although, given the agility and nimbleness her weapon demands, perhaps you shouldn't be surprised.

The ones who come next, they could be the problem.

"S-slowly now, okay...?"

"Please don't shake the ladder...!"

Female Bishop's difficulties you can understand, what with the trouble with her eyes, but your cousin's bumbling descent gets on your nerves. You don't intend to complain aloud—you know this isn't the sort of thing either of them was taught to do—but you will have to try to think of some way to help them for the next time this comes up.

You don't think it's really that far down, but the girls' movements on the ladder are slow and hesitant. You call out that it's all right, that you'll catch them if they fall, but it doesn't seem to help very much.

"I think it's *falling* they're afraid of. Doesn't matter if they'll be fine at the end," Myrmidon Monk notes.

You see he's right. It seems so obvious when he says it. You shake your head hopelessly and decide to take a look around.

You seem to be on the first square of a hallway, and there's no sense that any monsters are about to burst out at you. The real question is *where* on the second floor you are. The dungeon may go many levels deep, but nothing says it was necessarily dug straight down. Judging purely by the number of steps on a side, it seems to be built roughly in the shape of a square, but you don't know if this level is located directly beneath the one above or not…

"S-sorry about that. We're here now…"

"Phew, we *made* it…"

That would be Female Bishop and your *second* cousin arriving. Female Bishop is nodding slightly, but your *second* cousin has since collapsed on the ground. You remark with an amused smile that it makes her look sloppy, and she puffs out her cheeks at you. "Not all of us were allowed to spend our time climbing trees back home!"

So she thinks she would be on equal terms with you if she'd been allowed to clamber through branches all her life? You shake your head at this sore loser–ness of hers, then ask Half-Elf Scout what he thinks of the situation.

"Eh, that's the difference between a warrior and a magic user, I guess." He slides down to the second floor with hardly a sound, a thief in his element. He does a quick check of his equipment, then nods. "Great. And as your level goes up, the gap gets bigger, too, so I wouldn't sweat it too much."

"See? *That's* what you're missing!" your cousin says, apparently heartened by the scout's considerate remark and looking to make an attack of opportunity. "Right?" she adds, looking to Female Bishop for confirmation, but the other woman only shifts nervously. "Us girls have picked up some new tricks from that spell book, so don't underestimate us!" She puffs out her generous chest, full of confidence, and you have to admit that it won't hurt to have some more magic available.

You cut through the chatter to tell everyone it's about time to move out, and then you refocus your attention. It's time to explore the second floor—and confront the scruffy men.

They don't know you're coming or that you even exist, but then again, neither of you is compelled to be in this fight. When adventurers and monsters clash in this dungeon, all that awaits is victory for one and the Death for the other.

"So which way first?" Myrmidon Monk asks. You think about it for a moment, then conclude that wherever they are, the scruffy men can't be far. They might be no different from monsters now, but they'll still want to make their base somewhere that offers them the most convenience. If they're preying on adventurers exploring the first floor, then they would probably stay as close to here as possible.

"Agreed. Assuming there aren't any other stairways or the like around, of course."

If you're right about this, then that's another mystery of the maze you've solved. With the scruffy men hurt by the attack from the Knight of Diamonds and his party, you can't miss the opportunity this day represents. There's no way the enemy escaped unscathed; they must be injured as well.

You can't give them any time to lick their wounds or to relocate their base deeper into the dungeon in fear of reprisals. And on the unlikely possibility that the scruffy men dealt with the Knight of Diamonds before he and his party could even scratch them...

Well, it's too bad, but your adventure will end here. That's all there is to it.

"C'mon, Cap—let's get a move on. I'll bet those guys have a tidy little treasure hoard, too." Half-Elf Scout grins. You nod at him, then call to the others to form up. Female Bishop and your cousin both seem to have gotten their breathing under control, and you think they're going to be fine.

You form your ranks the same way as always, and then your friends and you start down the wire-frame hallway of the dungeon.

"North, one, two..." Female Bishop has the sheepskin map open; you can hear her pencil scratching along it, high-pitched above the sound of her footsteps.

You think of yourself as a relatively experienced explorer by now, but the dungeon is so much quieter than you ever thought. There are more urgent moments and less urgent ones, but at the very least, it isn't the constant, unyielding struggle you once imagined. You can't let down your guard, but if you're in a constant state of extreme vigilance, you'll be too fatigued when the moment that really requires you to pay attention comes along. To help avoid this, you look back over your shoulder and remark that you're given to understand there are no goblins on the second floor.

"Heh-heh… Well, small blessings, I guess," Female Bishop says with a mixture of reluctance and relief, her pencil stopping in her hand. "I'm glad we won't see any down here, but they're still there, up on the first floor…"

They aren't gone. That makes sense. You hadn't thought about it that way.

Then again, monsters seem to spring up endlessly from this dungeon, and that includes goblins. If you want to get all the goblins out of the dungeon, you'll have to confront the Death on the lowest floor.

"That makes sense…" She echoes your words in a whisper, dead earnest. "I hadn't thought about it that way…"

Female Warrior tugs on your sleeve unexpectedly. "Hey, how about slimes? What do you think?" You don't even look at her but say flatly that you have no idea. You hear a "grrr" and assume she's puffed out her cheeks. The sound is very pointed. "Aren't you being a bit cold?"

"Don't mind him," Half-Elf Scout says with a guffaw from the back row. "The cap just isn't that interested in stuff he's already decided to kill."

This time it's your turn to be a little annoyed. You wish he wouldn't talk about you like you were some sort of sword devil. Openly pleased by your reaction, Female Warrior turns to your scout and asks, "What about you?"

"Good question," he says. He thinks about it for a second before replying nonchalantly, "Slimes and goblins never carry that much cash, so I guess I'm not that interested in 'em, either, eh?"

"In other words, you're after money. Not what I'd call the highest of principles."

"Well, now…" Half-Elf Scout deliberately trails off. Female Warrior giggles.

"Hmm," muses your cousin, who has been listening to all this chatter with a smile. "Personally, I'd welcome an encounter with some humanoid monsters—it would give us a chance to try out our new spells…"

"That's true," agrees Female Bishop softly. "We did go to all that trouble to learn them."

"Well, isn't it nice to have you two along," Female Warrior says in a singsong voice and gives a nimble flourish of her spear. You likewise come to a stop, feeling out the footing ahead with the tiptoes of your sandals.

"Looks like you're out of luck," Myrmidon Monk clacks, drawing his short, bent blade from the scabbard hanging at the small of his back.

Just down the hall from where you've all stopped, the corridor is full of some kind of vapor of an unsettling color. The way it moves, though, is clearly organic—a wandering monster!

"Can we… Can we really cut that stuff or stab it…?" Female Warrior asks, and you don't blame her.

Your path is blocked by several roiling clouds of gas. Their color hints at their poisonous nature, and there's clearly more than one of them— What do you call a group of clouds of gas? A herd? They're obviously alive, yet they're just as obviously not normal organic life-forms but something created by magic. That means it's not immediately apparent whether blades and clubs will do any damage to them.

"Sorry," your cousin says, "I don't think my new magic is going to do much against these…"

You tell her not to worry about it, then draw your sword. You grasp the hilt in both hands, taking a deep, low stance and advancing step by sliding step. No one weapon, be it a blade or a spell or anything else, is effective against everything you might encounter. If your physical attacks don't work, then you'll have to rely on your cousin and Female Bishop for their magic. Why get upset with them just because their newest spells won't have any effect?

You shoot a glance at Female Warrior and Myrmidon Monk; then with a great shout, you charge in. You drop your torso low, kick one foot back, and strike upward from below. Your katana neatly slices the cloud of gas, sliding through it as easily as if you were cutting air. Without a pause, you bring your sword back, rising up again even as your eyes widen.

It works!

A bit of the gas drifts away like a cloud in the sky. The thing even spasms like a flesh-and-blood creature being cut!

"This might actually work…!" Female Warrior says, then drives at the enemy with her spear in one hand.

But just as you're getting used to the fact that you don't feel the creatures under your blade, one of them expands dramatically.

"CLOOOOOUDDDD!!!!"

It doesn't sound like a cry so much as an angry torrent of wind. But the moment the vapors surround your head, you involuntarily drop to your knees. You struggle for breath as if you are being strangled; you feel your life seeping away with every attempt to suck in oxygen. Your face burns, and you know you're being attacked by the living gas.

You flail your arms, waving away the mist, and the cold air of the dungeon rushes into your lungs.

"Take this!" Female Warrior rushes past you where you kneel coughing and choking, taking up a position ahead of you. With a sweet but fearsome yell, she drives her spear forward; you can hear it whoosh through the air. It scatters the gas cloud, but your opponent isn't going to take this lying down. Droplets of the dispersed mist fly every which way, and some of them land on Female Warrior's face.

"Hrr—agh?!" she gasps and reels backward. Seeing how pale she is, you pause in surprise even though you're in the middle of a battle.

Poison gas!

"I-it's okay… I'm fine!" Female Warrior retreats, supporting herself on her spear, but you distinctly acknowledge that she did nod at you. In the back row, your cousin and Female Bishop are hurrying to make a move, but you hold up your hand to stop them.

"Watch out!" Myrmidon Monk calls. "The monsters down here aren't like the ones on the first floor!" He holds his dagger in a reverse grip, while with his other hand, he forms the sigil of the god of wind—the Trade God. *"My god the roaming wind, let all on our road be good fortune!"*

At that instant, the wind stops. The gas clouds' movements become noticeably slower: This is the Silence miracle, a blessing of wind avoidance. You certainly don't need any other spells now. You see what Myrmidon Monk meant; this is a very different way of handling enemies from what you're used to. But…

You draw your sword back to your shoulder, then step toward the cloud, at the same time bringing your weapon down from high overhead.

"CDDLOOOUDD?!?!?!"

But they're weak.

With that one great slash, the gas clouds disappear like a bit of morning mist. The fog that had ensconced the hallway clears, and coins come falling to the ground with metallic *clink*s. Perhaps the coins formed the nucleus of the spell that gave these creatures life.

And so you survive this random battle without too much worry or fuss.

§

This is a good sign as far as it goes, but one could argue it's a bad sign, too.

Thus you muse to yourself as you give a precious antidote to Female Warrior. She grimaces. "I'm not a big fan of bitter stuff…"

Even here in a remote corner of the dungeon, you can still make a circle with holy water and set up camp. You can't count on it holding for very long, of course, but it will be enough for a short rest. You look around at your companions, catching their collective breath inside the circle, then place the bottle, drunk empty, on the floor.

"Hey, here, try some of this baked treat I got at the inn. It's delicious!"

"Oh, don't mind if I do, then… Thank you."

Your cousin is sharing provisions with Female Bishop; despite some fatigue, they still seem to have plenty of vitality.

You do need a little rest: You've come all the way from town, through the first floor and now some distance along the second, a fairly lengthy bout of exploration. Still, you haven't used up any spells. And you haven't forgotten the ones you committed to memory, so no problems there.

"Man, with all these random encounters, there's nothing for me to do!" crows Half-Elf Scout, who has been making up part of the back row. He idly plays with his dagger to pass the time but cackles to himself. His only real job is to keep an eye out behind you, and while that's a tremendously important role, it doesn't consume much stamina. Although it's true he can't let his attention waver. In that respect, he's pacing himself well… "Eh, no big deal. Never know when there might be a hidden doorway somewhere anyway." He must have noticed you watching him, because he grins. You nod back at him.

"Phew……"

It's really Female Warrior and yourself who concern you more than anything else. Your ability to concentrate isn't limitless. At the moment, Female Warrior is sitting down, leaning listlessly on her spear, looking somewhat spent. If you were to ask whether she's tired, you suspect she would insist that she's fine. Or maybe she would give that belly laugh of hers and say, *Yeah, a bit.*

Whichever it might be, you doubt she would tell you how she's really feeling. You need to make a decision. You all survived the battle on the first floor, and now you've obtained your first victory on the second. So that's a good sign—but your diminished stamina might not bode so well for the next battle.

You're startled from your thoughts by the sound of a pair of mandibles clacking. "If you think it's too dangerous, the answer's simple: retreat," Myrmidon Monk says, glancing at you. "Just like the others."

You indicate your agreement with Myrmidon Monk. It's worth remembering that you and Female Warrior aren't the only ones in the front row. He's here, too. It would be silly to rely on him to do everything, but to never let him do anything would be equally foolish; it would defeat the point of including him in the party. You remark that in the case of a retreat, you'd have to play rock-paper-scissors to decide who ended up as the rear guard, but he shrugs and doesn't say anything.

"………?" Rather unexpectedly, Female Bishop looks up, her nose twitching.

"Something wrong?" your cousin asks, looking at her with puzzlement, but she replies, "Oh, no." Your cousin picks a few crumbs from around Female Bishop's mouth. Maybe Female Bishop can sense her pop one into her own mouth, because she blushes and looks down. "It's just… Don't you think it smells a little like…blood?"

"Might be right," Half-Elf Scout says. "That knight we saw up top could have survived, but there's been an awful lot of killing down here, don't you think?" He seems to mean that even though you rarely encounter other adventurers in the dungeon, traces often remain. You try to chase away the image of a pile of dead adventurers in the rogues' hideout.

That's actually a rather good sign, you conclude. You've cut your way through those gas clouds, and now you're approaching the rogues' base. A safe step in the right direction is one of the best things you can hope for in the dungeon. After all, how often do those steps reveal a pit trap that you tumble into? You don't know anything about the terrain down here anyway. Might as well rely on Female Bishop's intuition.

"You're counting on me, sir?" she asks with a frown, but then she grips the sword and scales all the more tightly. "Okay, I understand."

She nods, and Myrmidon Monk says simply, "Let me take over the map."

The Trade God is the god of the wind, the god of travel, and perhaps that would make him the god of maps as well. Myrmidon Monk responds to your suggestion with a clack of his mandibles. Perhaps that's all the answer you need.

After a moment to compose yourself, you give the despondent-looking Female Warrior a pat on the shoulder. She looks up at you distantly for a second, then says "Yeah" with a small nod. "You're right… The things down here don't seem that different from the things upstairs, but…"

She gets to her feet, spear in hand, and the others likewise start gathering up their equipment and getting ready to go. You check one another, making sure armor and weapons are good to go. You help, needless to say. A leader's actions are what show that he's taking proper care of his party members and help put everyone's minds at ease.

"Have to say, the enemies down here make the skin crawl." The unexpected whisper in your direction comes from Myrmidon Monk. In addition to his monk's robes, he carries the characteristic curved blade of his people at his hip and always looks ready for battle. You clasp the palm that earlier patted the sopping shoulder of Female Warrior and ask if he means slimes.

"Yes... Well, no," Myrmidon Monk adds, his mandibles clacking and his face serious. "It's the Gas Clouds."

So that's what you call those roiling clouds of poisonous fumes. He frowns. You can tell yourself the omens look good as many times as you like, but the fact remains that you were caught unawares. If those things are the foot soldiers of the second floor of the dungeon, whosoever might have put them to the task...

"This is more than just a simple question of level," Myrmidon Monk says. "Those things aren't normal organic life-forms."

Well, that much is certainly true. Up on the first floor, the wandering monsters mostly consisted of things like goblins, slimes, animated corpses, and skeleton warriors. Then you come down to the second floor, and all of a sudden there are living clouds of gas floating around. And they spray poison, just to make things extra interesting...

'Ah. This isn't going to be straightforward.'

"Exactly. And we haven't been granted any miracles yet for healing poison or curing sickness. Don't let your guard down."

"What's the big deal? The cap took 'em out like they weren't even there," Half-Elf Scout says lightly, coming to tell you he's done getting his gear ready. You look him over and see that his leather armor and dagger both look to be in fine repair—no problems as far as you can tell. If you thought he simply painted his equipment black, you are surprised by the earthy dark-red hue the gear actually is. For the first time since you started working with him, you realize the color must meld better with darkness than actual black.

"If you can cut 'em up and they die, then no biggie. Nothing to worry about."

You grin and say he's exactly right, but your cousin butts in from behind:

"You know there are some creatures that can only be defeated with magic, right?"

Your cousin would go down for the count pretty much immediately if she had to engage in actual, physical combat, and you both know it. So instead, she's equipped with the absolute minimum of defensive gear, along with the staff she grips tightly. But nonetheless, of course, even if you aren't checking your spell caster's equipment, you have to make sure they look physically and psychologically fit.

You nod and indicate *No problem*; beside you, Half-Elf Scout looks at your cousin with exaggerated but utmost seriousness. "Welp, we'll just have to count on you if we meet one of those," he says.

"Heh-heh, gladly. And not me alone...remember?" Your cousin smiles and puts a hand on Female Bishop's shoulder. Female Bishop says, "That's right," but sounds nervous, not very convinced. She clutches at her sword and scales with fresh seriousness, though, and as she starts to walk, she cuts an inspiring figure. Your lips relax into a smile when you see her, and then you address the group:

'Let's go.'

Back in formation, you step outside the circle of holy water and resume your exploration. You follow the white wire-frame walls extending out into the darkness, one step at a time, ever deeper into the maze. Each time you come to a corner, Female Bishop stops and thinks, focusing carefully, then tells you where to go.

"To the right, I think..."

In this unfamiliar place, there are no other markers to rely on. The rest of you follow her without question. Taking your cue from Female Bishop behind you, who must be focusing her senses very carefully, you take an experimental sniff of the air.

The obvious question is what people actually mean when they talk about a someone or something's presence. Elves and wizards might see things invisible to others, but to your mundane human eyes, the world appears unremarkable. The only thing you can see at this moment is the wire-frame dungeon extending endlessly into the darkness before you.

Surely, then, even the most sensitive people can't pick up on something as convenient as presence. You need instead to pay attention to sounds, the shifts of the wind, odors, shadows, the coming and going of your own breath. And when you really focus, you find that no matter how long and how carefully you attend, there's little information to be had. "Where there's no smell, there's no taste," as the proverb has it—it's all *no*, nothingness. Even the stench of death that pervades a chamber after a battle is like this: Take one step outside the room, and you can no longer smell it. You have to simply force yourself to not let your mind wander and to think only of moving forward through the dark.

The way Female Bishop uses her intuition to help you—"To the right." "Left, I think."—is truly impressive. It's almost as if she perceives a different world than you do. Or maybe it's a natural talent. Maybe this slight and luckless girl was given a gift. An ability to sense whatever it is that hides down here in the dungeon. Whether that be monsters slinking through the dark, something threatening destruction upon the world from the deepest depths, or rogues. Each time you encounter such things down here, what awaits is not merely victory or defeat but death for either you or the other. So perhaps the nothing that creeps along your tongue is the flavor of the Death…

You smile at yourself and shake your head, pushing away the thought. You have to be careful. It's almost like you're getting hypnotized by the Death.

Battle is all but unavoidable if you enter a room, while out in the halls you never know when you might encounter a wandering monster. And if it's unavoidable, then there's no need to worry about it before it happens.

At the thought, you suddenly feel light, like your breath is finally reaching some deep part of your body that had been too stiff to accept it before. You need to worry less about invisible threats and more about the uncharacteristically reticent Female Warrior.

"………"

Ever since you determined to take on those rogues, she's been prone to bouts of gloom. You have no intention of prying into her inner life, but if that gloom blunts the tip of her spear, that would be a problem.

So what to do…?

"Oh, that's right," says a cheery voice completely at odds with your own concerns. It is, needless to say, your cousin, who digs industriously through a bag slung over her shoulder. "I found some terrific

candy in town. I'm not sure about this walking-along-in-silence nonsense, so maybe we could all share it."

Blasted *second* cousin. This would have been a lot more appropriate
during your little break earlier.

Your cousin effectively ignores your "advice," smiling brightly as she
passes around a bag with little balls of candy in it. Not wanting to be the
wet blanket, you take one and pop it in your mouth but immediately frown.

'It's mint.'

"Aw, bad luck, Cap," Half-Elf Scout says with a grin, rolling his own
candy around in his mouth. He's quick. He must have gotten some
sweet flavor. You purse your lips and say something unkind; Half-Elf
Scout glances off to one side without breaking his smile. You follow
his look to discover Myrmidon Monk standing there with the bag
in his hand and a look of chagrin on his face.

"…Mint," he says.

'Yeah, that's right.' You nod.

Myrmidon Monk slowly shakes his head. "I think I'll pass for now…
This would be a bad time to be distracted by my mouth."

'Oh yeah? Well, that's what it is, then.'

"You're right about that," he responds gravely.

"I think I'll pass, too, then," Female Bishop says, observing Myrmidon Monk's reaction closely.

"Are you sure?" your cousin asks, looking disappointed. "I think
they're really good…"

"I'll try one after we're finished, then," Female Bishop tells her, and
this gets your cousin smiling again. She trots over to Female Warrior
and holds out the bag, smiling brightly. "How about you, milady?"

"Huh…?" Female Warrior looks taken aback, though you can't
imagine she's actually caught off guard. She glances at you uncertainly, and you nod. Your cousin just keeps smiling. Finally, Female
Warrior, looking a bit resigned—or is that hesitant?—reaches slowly
for the bag. "…Any strawberry-flavored ones?"

"There sure are! Uh, let's see… This one, I think!"

'You think.' Your teasing earns you only an "It's too dark to be sure!"
from your cousin. Well, if nothing else, avoid the white ones and you
won't get mint.

At that suggestion, you hear Myrmidon Monk mumble, "I didn't even think of that," and Half-Elf Scout laughs.

"I think mint is good, too," Female Bishop says politely, and you feel your cheeks work into a smile.

Encouraged, perhaps, by the convivial atmosphere, Female Warrior reaches into the bag and pops one of the balls of candy into her mouth. "…Mm, it's so sweet." A happy look comes over her face, and you exhale pointedly.

Bah. This is why you can't win with that cousin of yours.

For the next few minutes, the only sound is candy rolling around in people's mouths. By the time there's only the last traces of mint left on your tongue, you find yourself standing in front of a deep, dark door.

§

"…It ain't locked. No traps, neither, is my guess," Half-Elf Scout concludes after carefully investigating the door with the tools that normally hang at his belt. Despite his characteristic tone and attitude, he's actually quite a diligent person. You don't believe he would make a mistake on a matter like this.

You nod in acknowledgment, then touch the door with one gloved hand. The metal portal is essentially indistinguishable from the door to every other chamber you've seen; it's all a little too neat. Not that you have any reason to doubt Female Bishop, but you wonder if the rogues are really in here.

This dungeon is very strange.

You know there was a battle here not long ago at all, yet the maze hides any lingering miasma or other traces of it. This might be the very place where the Knight of Diamonds and his party fought just this morning, but there's no way to be sure.

"…This is it. The smell of blood, I think it's…" But Female Bishop can't be certain, either, and she trails off.

"Well, only one way to find out," Myrmidon Monk says with a shrug. He draws his curved blade and holds it in a reverse grip, ready to go. "Let there be monsters or rogues or whatever in there. Makes no difference to me."

"True that," Half-Elf Scout says, matching Myrmidon Monk's unconcerned manner, but it's Female Warrior you're worried about.

When you ask if she's good to go, she replies ambivalently, "Well…" But then she gives a twirl of her spear and continues. "…Yeah, I'm fine. Shall we?" There's a *crack* as she bites through the last of her candy.

Good.

You nod briefly, then draw your beloved blade from its place at your hip. Even here in the gloom of the dungeon, it seems to sparkle; it may be nameless, but it's yours. You work a little spit into the hilt, then hold the sword low and turn toward the door.

"Here we go…," your cousin says quietly. She sounds nervous, yes, but also somehow relaxed—just like usual. "You have some kind of plan?"

The edges of your lips curl up, and you declare theatrically:

'Think we know what to do by now. Let's get started.'

And then you kick the door as hard as you can, smashing it in before you charge into the chamber bellowing your name as a battle cry. The rest of the party piles in after you.

"The hell?!"

"Back for more, ya filthy adventurers?"

You seem to have surprised the room's inhabitants—the scruffy men!

Now, standing in the room, you can finally smell it: a stench of blood strong enough to turn your stomach. You don't think even the most rundown tavern in the city would smell quite this bad. At your feet are the remains of some unidentifiable meal and a stewpot in which bones and loot appear to coexist.

The enemies—how many are there? You take a sweeping glance across the room, evaluating the situation.

"Th-the hell are you doing here?!" One of the men scrambles to his feet, awkwardly raising a dagger seemingly before he's had time to think about what he's doing.

He's finished.

You take a step forward, planting your foot on a reddish-brown splotch on the floor, then close the distance with another step before bringing your sword down from overhead.

"Eeyargh!" The silver flash slices into the man's neck, severing blood vessels and producing a spray of gore. His breath makes a whistling from his demolished throat for a moment before he collapses to the ground. No matter how good you are, what's unprotected by your armor is still unprotected. You can't afford to show any openings in battle.

You let the momentum of your strike transition into a flick to get the blood off your sword; then you proceed to the center of the room. There's only one door. That means the exit is behind you. You need to take up a position here so that not one of them can escape!

"Just leave this to me…!" Female Warrior flits past you, her spear lashing out like an extension of her arms.

"Hrgh?!" The sharp spear tip leaps upward like a snake, piercing one of the rogues through the throat. With a *whoosh*, the spear tears sidelong out of his neck, and Female Warrior takes up another stance, gripping the spear with both hands. That's two down. Another six to go—no, wait…

"Huh, damn! First those other guys, now you… Busy day today."

Whoosh. A giant of a man stands up in the shadows at the back of the room. He's a veritable barbarian; you're startled to see chain mail glitter on his body, while in his hand is a broadsword.

Must be their chief.

You slide forward, gauging your distance, while you shift your katana into a low position. You assume this is an experienced opponent. He looks nonchalant, but he must know what he's doing to have gathered this band of brigands around him. That makes seven opponents altogether. They outnumber you. And when you consider their levels…

"I've got your back," Myrmidon Monk says calmly by way of encouragement. His knife, still in a reverse grip, parries a blow from one of the foes as he moves into position in the front row. You give him the slightest nod, then glance quickly back over your shoulder. Half-Elf Scout is standing there glaring at the rogues with his dagger at the ready, guarding the spell casters. Female Bishop holds up her sword and scales nervously, while beside her, your cousin brandishes her short staff and winks.

"Buy us some time…!" she whispers.

But of course.

You take a deep breath to steady yourself, count the squares to judge the distance, then stare at the chief.

"Huh, three men and three women. Nice stuff—after all, a man gets hungry after a fight!" The one you assume is the leader hefts his broadsword and grins menacingly at you. Then, with lust dripping from his voice, he howls loud enough to shake the stones: "You know the drill, boys! Rip off their heads and then have your way with 'em!"

A collective shout rises from the others, and you hear a great scraping of equipment.

The room isn't that big. Even if they all attack at once, the seven of them won't be able to reach you at the same time. So long as Female Warrior and Myrmidon Monk can hold up their ends, you're not afraid of any attacks reaching the back row. And if by chance one does, Half-Elf Scout is there to intercept it and hold the line.

How do you know he'll do that? Because it's his job. And your job is...

"What say we get started, eh...!"

To keep this brute busy for every move, every second it's possible to wring out of him.

§

You can tell from the moment the weapon rises in the air that the blow coming at you from dead ahead is going to be a big one. A sword can survive being chipped, but you can't let it get bent. You meet the massive hatchet with the back of your blade and step to one side.

Your hand tingles. It's obvious you can't take these attacks head-on. Unless of course you want to die with the hilt of your own sword buried in your forehead.

Shf. Your straw sandals slide over stones stained with many battles' worth of blood and gore, and you take a breath.

He's experienced.

"Hoo, not bad!"

Now you see. You should have expected as much from the leader of a party, even a party of rogues. Everything he wears reeks of blood and rust. His mail sparkles. Then there's the giant hatchet. All look like they've seen many battles. It could just be a bluff, of course. But the massive stature of the man in the mail suggests otherwise.

Recognizing that it's going to be a tough fight, you carefully scan the room.

"Yah!" Beside you, Female Warrior, sounding incongruously cheerful, puts her spear to work. They always tell beginners not to use a spear in an enclosed space, but apparently, one of these chambers doesn't count. The weapon is like a living thing in Female Warrior's petite hands; it shoots back and forth, jumps up and down, sweeps through the air.

"Grgh?!"

"C'mon! Surround her! Get in close enough and she can't swing at you!"

"Oh, I don't know about that." By this point, she seems to be doing less stabbing and more beating her opponents with the haft of her weapon, but anyway...

"Not sure you have time to admire her work," Myrmidon Monk says. "Though I admit, she is distractingly competent."

And you definitely don't have time to look back at what's happening with the magic. As long as you keep the rogues off the back row, that's enough. You catch an intake of breath from your cousin. Female Bishop is silent. You need them to focus on their spells, so you don't want to give them any unnecessary distractions. You track your opponent's movements with your eyes, sliding to keep yourself between him and the spell casters.

The giant man leans the broadsword across his shoulder as if it were a toy, his eyes glinting with bestial malice. When he grins at you, revealing crooked teeth, he looks almost like any other wandering monster you might find in the dungeon. "I'll grind your bones to make my bread—ha!" he says. "That's just a little joke. Don't want you getting the wrong idea—I'm a gentleman; I really am."

You don't take your eyes off the resting broadsword. The thing is massive. It should be easy enough to tell when he's going to swing it—*should* be.

Hadn't you heard a proverb about how big heads have small wit?

Turns out life is not nearly that convenient. The man's strength is precisely in his *strength*; his muscles are his power. Not something to be underestimated.

"Precisely."

The blow comes almost before your brain can process it. The broadsword seems like nothing more than a flash of light.

You raise your sword over your head—the image of the wounded knight flashes through your mind—then you angle the sword vertically and press your hand against the spine.

There's a tang of metal on metal!

Your hands feel as if an electric shock has run through them, and your ears ring loudly. You reel back as if struck by a hammer, but then you force your feet to stay steady under you.

That was no cleaving strike. It was a sidelong swipe meant to take off your head—and a critical hit at that!

"—!" Your cousin calls your name from behind you, but you can't quite seem to hear her. But still you nod. You can do that much. You're alive. So there's no problem.

That one second, that instantaneous vision of the Knight of Diamonds with the wound to his neck, saved your life.

"Huh, that's two of you I didn't manage to kill today with that move. Maybe I'm getting old." The man in the mail works his arms in a circle. You spare a glance at your katana. It isn't broken, or bent, or even chipped. Good.

There probably won't be another attack like that.

A sideswipe disguised as an overhead blow. A brilliant move but the sort of thing that works only once.

Now all you have to do is keep whittling away at his hit points. Still, a person can always die from a single, straight hit. Although that's as true of the enemy as it is of you...

"Hrrrahhh!!"

The broadsword crashes toward you again, and with a quick, sliding step, you slip out of the way. You don't know how many toe-to-toe exchanges you could hold on for before your sword would just be batted out of the way. You can still feel a tingling in your hands from the last one. But you can't play a purely defensive game, either. You have to go on the attack. You need to attack to attain victory, and to attain victory, you need to kill.

Even as you step away, you pull your katana down into a low position, sliding back and to the right. You'll never be able to cut through the mail the man is so ostentatiously wearing. Your targets are the legs, the arms, the flanks, and the neck.

The moment the man draws his broadsword back, you advance. You put your weight forward ever so slightly, using the momentum to bring your sword up on a diagonal, stretching out with your arms as you go.

"Heh…!"

There's a ringing as the blade scrapes the mail. You feel no real resistance. Your opponent has used the momentum from his broadsword swing to get back out of the way. It instantly proves that he fully understands the strengths and weaknesses of his weapon and has adapted his fighting style to accommodate them. But you don't care. So have you.

Your katana has bounced off your enemy at a diagonal, but rather than bring it back to center, you relax your right hand and twist your left, flipping the blade around. You press forward again, hoping to bring the sword down on the man's neck.

But your blow is deflected by his broadsword, which he brings up on a diagonal. It's a textbook move, escaping the line of attack by swinging to the outside. Without hesitation, you pull your sword back, and you see that the man's next strike will come up from below.

You jump.

You pull your feet in as close to your body as you can, leaping *over* the broadsword. You know the man's weapon is unsuited to executing a series of quick strikes, so you realize you're unlikely to be hit between when you launch yourself into the air and when you land back on the ground.

But the enemy knows it, too. By the time your feet touch the stone floor, your vision is full of the man's fist.

That broadsword strike was one-handed?! You crouch down deep to minimize the impact of your landing and neatly dodge the punch.

This is bad. You can feel the rush of wind from the force of the punch above your head; you somersault backward and out of range. The broadsword crashes down where you were just a second before. The stone floor cracks under the impact.

You jump to your feet and bring your katana up in front of you, your breath coming in small, short gasps that make your shoulders heave. You force yourself to breathe more calmly, releasing the stiffness from your body, cooling the heat, urging the blood that seems to have rushed to your head to flow back to the rest of you.

Sweat runs into your eyes, but you can't afford to blink. Thanks to the sharkskin wrapping around the hilt of your sword, at least you aren't afraid that your hands will slip. You feel as if you should be hearing the clangor of battle around you, but it no longer reaches your ears. Your field of vision narrows until the man in the mail seems to occupy your entire world.

"Har! Har! Har!" the man thunders. "Looks like you're running out of tricks!"

But that's fine, you think. Because…

"*Musica!* Music—"

"*Concilio!* United—"

"*Terpsichore!* With dance!"

Because the same goes for him!

"Hrgh! Wha—?!"

The two girls intone the Dance spell in ringing, clear voices. By the time the man in the mail notices them, it's too late. His feet start to spasm almost like he's dancing but out of his control. It lasts for only a second. Still, that's all the time you need. You take a horse spike you've drawn out of the hilt of your blade and recite three words of power as you throw it.

'*Sagitta quelta raedius.*'

In other words: Magic Missile!

"Hyargh!"

The spike, imbued with total accuracy, as if it had been loosed by a master archer, buries itself deep in the man's eye. He stumbles back, his hand to his face. Now you don't have to worry about that broadsword.

'*Ryaaahhh!*'

You let loose a great war cry, close the distance between the two of you in a flash, and bring your sword down from high over your head. The blade slides easily into the crevice between the man's neck and his shoulder.

"Grgh—hrgh?!"

You can feel it under your hands. The spray of blood shows you've found a vital point. The giant man gags as if choking on his own blood, and shortly thereafter, he crumples to the ground. The broadsword clatters from his limp hands.

"We… We did it! We did it!" your cousin whoops. Gods. You always knew it was really her you should be afraid of.

"Y-yes," Female Bishop says. Your cousin takes her hand and exclaims happily, seemingly oblivious to the profound power of her own spell.

You give your faithful sword a shake to get the blood off and look around.

"Hell, even I could've killed a guy who had his feet pulled out from under him," Myrmidon Monk says, casually eviscerating the throat of the man in front of him. It's no doubt thanks to Myrmidon Monk that none of the giant man's friends interfered with your fight. You thank him for his help, then quickly reassume a fighting stance. Four enemies left?

"…If you're going to thank me, do it later," Myrmidon Monk adds with a clack of his mandibles. "This isn't over yet."

"He's right. Besides, I'll be wanting a little thanks myself," Female Warrior says with a laugh, her face flush as she drives her spear under an enemy's clavicle. The weapon finds its way through the chinks in the man's armor and has soon claims his life. Three left now.

"Looks like I won't have much to do till this is all over," Half-Elf Scout remarks nervously, the lighthearted comment an attempt to ease the tension he feels.

You just shrug, size up the remaining opponents—thrown into a panic by the loss of their leader—and then dive in.

§

"P-please spare me! I surrender! Y-yeah, that's it! I—I surrender...!!"

It's not long after that the last surviving opponent throws his rusty sword aside and begs for mercy. The sword skips across the greasy stone tiles noisily. You kick it away.

"I'm begging you! Spare me my life...! I swear I'll leave the dungeon; I'll never come back to this town...!"

There's no compulsion to treat bandits and rogues like human beings. Especially not ones who skulk around the dungeon like monsters.

You could save this highwayman's life. Or you could kill him. What to do? You let your sword rest low in one hand but always at the ready. You look at your companions.

"Hmm...," Female Warrior says.

"I don't care either way," Myrmidon Monk comments. Both of them recognize that the battle is over and appear to have relaxed. Half-Elf Scout simply shrugs and shakes his head. As for your cousin... Well, you think you can guess.

That just leaves...

"We ought to offer him salvation." Female Bishop is the last to speak, and when she does so, her voice is terribly calm, almost devoid of emotion. You raise an eyebrow as she shuffles forward, past you, raising her sword and scales with a ringing of metal. The bandit likewise regards the young woman who has appeared before him as if he can't quite believe what he's seeing. "If this man here truly has had a change of heart, then we can spare him his life. Nothing simpler."

Hmm, you grunt. Well, it's all the same to you. The battle has already been decided. You return your sword to its sheath, clicking it into place. Female Bishop smiles faintly and nods, then turns toward you with a swirling motion.

That's when the bandit grins, baring his teeth, and leaps up with a dagger drawn from his pouch. "I've got you now, you damn—"

In the same instant, his head explodes with a sound not unlike a ripe tomato.

"And if he has not changed, then he is fit only for death."

Turning again with theatrical grace, Female Bishop pulls out the sword and scales with a flourish. The plates of the scales crashed into the man's head, splitting his skull open. There's a spray of blood and brains, almost artistic, across the wall, and you can hear your cousin suck in a breath.

"...I'm sorry to say, he made the choice himself." Female Bishop, still sounding completely calm, doesn't even spare a glance at the twitching corpse. The cold smile that comes across her cheek is flecked with blood.

Hmm, you grunt. Well, it's all the same to you. You would have been content either way.

After a moment's thought, you figure out what you want to say. "You look like you could hold your own in the front row."

"Heavens, me? Don't say such frightening things," Female Bishop responds, sounding once again like a young girl; a frown creases her face as if she's genuinely scared by the idea. You give her a light clap on the shoulder as a show of thanks, then motion to your cousin.

"Oh, uh... Right! Leave it to me!" You can hear nervousness and hesitation. But also vigor that overmatches them both. Your cousin hurries to Female Bishop. She offers her a word of appreciation for her effort, then gives her a waterskin and tactfully urges her to a corner of the room.

This is something about your cousin that you respect from the bottom of your heart.

"Hey... Are you all right?" As you watch the two women go off together, Female Warrior tugs on your sleeve. You shake your head and say that you don't know. At the very least, it's not so bad that you can't go on. People each have their own heartstrings, some more sensitive, some less, and sometimes emotions can flare. Perhaps the bandit's actions, the way he begged for his life, created such a moment for Female Bishop. When you consider the deep wounds she's suffered in her past, it's not hard to imagine. So long as she doesn't bring it up, though, you feel it's not your place to pry.

"You...," Female Warrior starts, and then she shakes her head, "do have your good side."

You shrug, then walk over to a pile of junk the bandits accumulated in a corner of the room. You tell Female Warrior you'll trust her to stand guard, to which she replies listlessly, "Yeah, sure." But you think it's all right. You have faith in her now.

©lac

Half-Elf Scout and Myrmidon Monk follow you to go through the assembled loot. Honestly—this is what keeps people coming back to hack and slash.

"It's how a man makes his money," Half-Elf Scout says. "Can't stop even if you wanted to."

'*That's how adventurers are.*' You nod at him, then reach a gloved hand into the pile.

"Pain in the ass," Myrmidon Monk clacks—but you thank the two of them. Because neither of them said anything about what Female Bishop did just a few moments ago. As the leader of the party, it's only natural that you should feel grateful to them for being considerate of another member.

They look at each other and then declare, almost in unison, ""Hey, it's nothing.""

You chuckle and drop the subject, determined to continue your exploration.

Everything you find—perhaps you ought to have expected this—is adventuring gear. Brand-new armor, weapons, empty pouches, and rank tags. You load all these things, one by one, into one of the hempen sacks you were given as body bags. These beasts seem to have eaten up every adventurer who was careless enough to venture too deep into the first floor. Literally, you suspect—for there is no way to get a proper meal down here in the dungeon. A look in the stewpot makes it all too clear what the men had been living off. Maybe, you think to yourself, what Female Bishop did was exactly the right thing.

As Myrmidon Monk mentioned, what you encountered here were not men but monsters.

"…Yo, Captain," Half-Elf Scout says suddenly. You look over to find him despondently holding a dirty cloth and some leather armor. The cloth seems to have served as a hair band; a few strands of golden hair still cling to it. The armor appears to have been white once, though you can hardly tell for the blood and gore splashed across it.

You recognize them both.

You glance back at Female Warrior, still keeping a vigilant watch, and at Female Bishop and your cousin just across from her. You can't catch what they're talking about. But you see your cousin giggle, and even Female Bishop's stiff face relaxes into a smile.

No special need to say anything.

Having made the decision, you toss the hair band and armor into the bag.

They just look familiar, that's all. There must be a million adventurers with golden hair or white armor. You murmur as much aloud, and Myrmidon Monk responds with a twitch of his antennae. "...I didn't see anything at all." *Clack, clack* go his mandibles, and then he makes a holy sigil in front of his chest. "May all those who died here be blessed with a fine wind."

You nod and stand. You've done all that needs to be done. You have no more business here.

Let's go.

"...Come on—let's get going," your cousin says to Female Bishop then. "It's been a hard day. We need to make sure we get a nice, long rest."

"Right. Right...," Female Bishop replies, and the two of them get to their feet. You turn your eyes toward Female Warrior, and much as you expected, you find her giggling with that ambiguous expression on her face.

You and your companions form up, then check one another's equipment. Nothing amiss. And no serious injuries, either. You nod your approval, then lead everyone out of the chamber, preparing to make your way back to the surface.

You say something to Female Bishop, who responds, "Oh, sorry," and quickly riffles through her belongings for the map. Her guidance is clear and sure, with no hint of hesitation, and you start to think this is going to be okay.

Thankfully, as you proceed from hallway to chamber, chamber to hallway, you don't encounter any wandering monsters. As you explore deeper and deeper into the dungeon, you're going to have to start taking the journey home into account. Every warrior, however experienced, has a limit to their strength and focus. Repeated battles wear away one's life. Even were it not so, how many chances does this Dungeon of the Dead really offer for life?

"I admit it was tough…," your cousin says suddenly, when you reach the top of the ladder leading from the second floor to the first. You've taken a very brief break to collect yourselves and have a drink. She's sat right down on the stone floor of the hallway and is smiling as if somehow relieved. "But now it's a little less dangerous for those girls to adventure, huh?"

'*Sure*' is all you say.

The surface is practically before your eyes now.

§

When you reach the entrance—the exit—of the dungeon, you find it filled with a gentle light, so different from the darkness below. Up in the sky, you see the stars and the twin moons shining. It is well into the night by now.

The royal knight on guard duty must sense something from your demeanor, because she simply bows silently to you. After all, she can't miss the blood-soaked bag you're carrying or the evidence of a major battle.

You just shrug at her as you go past, walking slowly along the road to town.

"Oof, man… Talk about tired…," Half-Elf Scout says.

"My feet are killing me. And I'm sweating from head to toe. I just want to wipe myself off…" Female Warrior groans miserably.

You nod at them; it's understandable. This was your first time down to the second floor, and you had to endure a huge battle, to boot. You don't believe you made any specific errors of judgment, but all the same, you're impressed that everyone was able to keep pace.

You could thank them from the bottom of your heart, or you could thank Fate and Chance for keeping everyone safe.

"…I know!" your cousin says, clapping her hands as she patters up to you with her face shining. "It's been such tough adventuring—why don't we take a little break tomorrow?"

"Wha—? But…" Female Bishop's face clouds over, and she looks at the others to see how they react.

Stupid second *cousin, always dropping these ideas out of the blue.*

You see that Female Bishop's face is clean; your cousin must have been kind enough to wipe off the blood spatter. Even so, the tinge of fretfulness is unmistakable, and you can feel her getting nervous again. "...Are you sure that's a good idea?" she asks.

"Well, we worked hard today. Didn't we?" your cousin says back, looking at you. You think about it for a moment, then nod and say it's probably all right. For one thing, everything you've heard suggests the pace of your party is considerably faster than those of most other adventurers. Although maybe that's because...

"Not a man jack of them cares about anything but making money. Not that it matters to me."

The remark Myrmidon Monk spit out is right.

All too few adventurers are truly interested in discovering the source of the Death that lurks in the depths of the dungeon.

The closer you get to town, the more ruddy-faced, grinning adventurers you see wearing ostentatious equipment. On some level, you could say those rogues were simply enthralled by the dungeon's riches, just like the rest. There are those enthralled by the Death, by this awful maze. They're like wandering monsters themselves, Non-Prayer Characters. That's why you must challenge the second floor and, someday, the third. And you need to take care of yourselves now if you're going to keep moving forward.

"True that," Half-Elf Scout says. "Heading into parts unknown while we're still rundown? That's a death wish if I ever heard one."

You're glad that he agrees. In any case, the goal for today is to simply get back to the inn. Selling the equipment you found (dead adventurers swing no swords) and delivering the rank tags to the temple can wait until tomorrow.

As you say all this, you register how tired you are yourself. Don't forget—you both fought and used magic today.

"I told you, rest is best."

It remains a mystery to you just why your cousin is grinning as brightly as she is. But as you return a tired smile, you can't help feeling...at home. It is the height of good fortune that you've encountered such rare and fine companions.

Full of the satisfaction of a job well done, you eventually collapse onto the pile of straw in the stables. You fully expect to sleep like a log tonight...

§

But ironically, complete exhaustion can actually make sleep lighter. Maybe some of the nerves of battle are still with you, because it seems like the slightest sound grates on your ears.

You sit up off the surprisingly comfortable pile of straw, picking bits of the stuff from your clothes. Half-Elf Scout, nearby, mumbles something in his sleep. Maybe Myrmidon Monk's finding it hard to settle down, too, because he's tossing and turning over in a corner of the stable.

Careful not to wake the others, you grab your beloved sword and slowly work your way outside. A pleasantly cool night breeze wafts a sweet aroma to your nostrils. Soap, perhaps. Is the fact that you can notice that a sign of how much your level has increased?

Now that you think about it, how long has it been since you came to this town? You've found excellent companions, adventured in the dungeon, and survived bouts of mortal combat. Each only represents a small bit of experience, but together they've really changed you.

"...And? Ever gonna talk to me?"

One of those priceless companions is standing just outside the stable. Female Warrior smiles at you, and, just as she once did, you beckon her to come take a seat on a pile of straw.

"Sure... Mm, soft as ever." She sits surprisingly lightly, then draws her knees up to her chin, looking pleased. "Say," she says, tilting her head like a child. "Were you hoping for something today?"

You smile and shake your head. *No.*

"Huh," she mumbles with disinterest.

But what, you wonder, is this about? Isn't she just as tired as you?

"Hmm? For some reason, the more tired I am, the more awake I feel." She obviously went right back to her room to clean herself off, because her hair is glistening. "I guess you could say I'm...killing time?"

Makes sense.

Both of you realize this conversation is no different than it was last night. So what comes next must be the same, too. You wait silently, expectantly.

"…Aw, who am I kidding? That's just an excuse…" She glances at you out of the corner of her eye and smiles faintly. "I thought maybe I should say thank you while I have the chance. Or something like that."

And you, just like the other night, look up at the moons shining in the sky and smile.

'Truth is, haven't done much to be thanked for.'

You made good on the responsibility you accepted when you became party leader, and you brought everyone home safely. That's really it—if anything, you should be thanking them.

You tell her all this as casually as you can.

"…True."

Female Warrior imitates you, looking up at the moons and squinting against the night breeze. For a while, neither of you says anything.

You could say something to her, or you could keep the silence. After a moment's thought, you tell her calmly that if there's anything she wants to talk about, she should feel free.

"Oh, very encouraging. I think you've been spending a bit too much time with a certain monk." She giggles, but you weren't really joking. You meant every word. If she wants to talk about something, she can certainly talk; if she doesn't want to, you don't intend to drag it out of her. You're happy to stay quiet if that's what she wants or to talk if she would prefer. It's not as if you have to know every detail of each other's stories to be companions or friends.

But—if you had to call it one way or the other, you would say she looks like she wants to talk. In fact, she just said she'd come to talk while she could, so she shouldn't be surprised that you're asking.

"Hmm…," Female Warrior murmurs noncommittally, her lips creasing into that teasing smile of hers. "I think you're just humoring me. Did you learn how from that big sister of yours?"

She's your *second* cousin, you insist. And this has nothing to do with her. It's purely a matter of your own personality.

"Okay—so say I don't want to talk?"

Then that will be what it will be. She can stay and watch the moons without a word or go back to her room and try to sleep. You return this answer as nonchalantly as possible.

Female Warrior watches you for a long moment, then finally, with a note of exasperation, says, "…Honestly. Sometimes I think I'm gonna go crazy talking to you…"

You don't say anything back, just shrug. Female Warrior sniffs and pouts. Finally, she continues. "Listen, I… I've always believed that what happens twice happens three times."

'What happens twice?'

"Mm." She nods. "Remember how when you met me, I was asking the temple to do some burials? Well…that was the second group."

You do remember she seemed immensely calm despite the fact that her party had just been destroyed. You had assumed it was an attitude born from deep experience with the dungeon, but even so, you were surprised.

"When I started out, you know, I had some…older sisters, you might call them. Girls from the same orphanage. We figured that if we were going to be adventurers, we should all start out together."

You've heard that's quite common. Those girls you met were the same way. Not unusual at all.

Of course, whether children or elderly, everyone faces the same conditions. You have to play the game with the cards you're dealt, win or lose with what is in your hand. Complain if you like—it won't change anything. The dice of Fate and Chance treat all equally. Even the gods.

"Well, I guess I had good luck, if nothing else.

"Got attacked by some bushwackers, and the older girls all died."

Female Warrior actually giggles a little as she says this; you can't imagine what's in her mind or her heart right now. She might be the only one who knows. You decide not to indulge in idle speculation.

"We thought, if there's a Death down in the dungeon, maybe there's a Life, too. But it didn't go so well, that…"

You can't judge the depth of feeling concealed in those whispered words.

The dead do not come back to life. That's one of the immutable rules of this Four-Cornered World. Even the Resurrection miracle performed by the clerics at the temple only calls life back from the cusp of death. Like the pips of the dice, death cannot be revoked or changed. If the possibility exists at all, it must rest only in some legacy from the Age of the Gods or perhaps in a divine miracle—a real one.

But if all that dwells in the depths of the dungeon is the Death—if it is something truly beyond human understanding—then she simply gambled on that tiny sliver of a chance.

"With everyone dying around me, I figured I had to get out of there quickly." If she dropped dead before she could bring them back, who would there be to resurrect her companions?

At this, a sly smile crosses your face, and you remark that that's a poor excuse. What are the chances of a newly minted adventurer getting out of the proving grounds alive? Of course, you figure she knows that better than you do.

"Sorry," Female Warrior says now with a catlike rasp in the back of her throat. "Ha-ha. It was just a joke. I made it up. Every word. Just thought I'd tease you a bit, that's all." She practically leaps to her feet. She kicks her long legs like a child playing a game. You don't get up. You simply watch her. You ask if she's feeling better.

"...Mn. I'm fine now. Thanks. I'm starting to want my bed, you know? ...Think I'll head back."

You might have tomorrow off, but you did go on an adventure today. Best to get some rest, you tell her. She just waves her hand over her shoulder as you watch her go...

"Oh, one more thing," she says. She turns back to you, and the gossamer moonlight paints her face a pale white as she whispers, "...This one's real." She giggles, and her face blossoms into a smile.

Before you can say anything back, she leaves the stables behind. You take care to make sure her name is held deep in your heart—not the number she bears but her real name. You won't let yourself forget it.

Now that you have a chance to think, you're startled by how much happened in the course of one day, one adventure.

The night is quiet again now that you're alone. The only sounds you hear are those that drift to you from the inn, the opening of the gate, and occasional footsteps.

You know well why the gates might open at this hour, why a crowd of people might come into the town. Another village or city somewhere has succumbed to the Death, the people there have lost their

©lack

homes, and at the end of their wanderings, they find themselves at this fortress city.

It's a strange thing.

Everyone seems to wind up here, even though this city is built hard upon the wellspring of the Death that threatens the world.

There's the loot that seems to flow endlessly from the dungeon. Whether you're an adventurer or merchant, you can make a living here. However listless your steps along the streets of the city might be, you may enter into the dungeon with a glimmer of hope. There you might be swallowed by the Death, never to return.

Suddenly caught up in this chilling thought, you grip your beloved sword in your hand especially hard.

What is the Death? What is the dungeon?

The only way to know is to delve deep and find out.

A white wisp of smoke curls into the sky from the dragon's mountain far away before it's borne off on the wind to who knows where.

AFTERWORD

Hullo, Kumo Kagyu here! Did you enjoy Volume 1 of *Dai Katana: The Singing Death*?

This was a story where adventurers delved into a dungeon and fought to the death with monsters, hoping to get ever farther. I poured my heart and soul into writing it, so I hope you had fun.

This book takes place long before *Goblin Slayer*. It's the tale of one very special party of adventurers who braved the deepest depths of the deepest dungeon this world knows.

This is an old world. An old adventure. There's a wire-frame dungeon, endless streams of monsters, and loot galore.

And there are adventurers who gather at the tavern. Death in the deeps of the dungeon. And the victory that awaits at the end of the long, slow accumulation of these things.

It's an old, old story, the sort of thing that might now be known chiefly from legends and songs.

As we've seen in *Goblin Slayer*, the Four-Cornered World is full of adventurers. And even more than that, it's full of adventures. There are fire-spewing mountains, evil wizards in their fortresses, the inn from hell, a dungeon full of deadly traps, the inn from hell…

Obviously, there's going to have to be more than a little goblin slaying going on here. The death that emanates from the dungeon, the monsters, demons, threats, wealth, treasure, and honor.

Killing a few goblins isn't going to save the world. And if the world ends before that village is destroyed, then it was all for nothing.

Of course, it's no spoiler to say that the world is saved in the end. We know that from *Goblin Slayer*. And you should all be aware that it happened thanks to some adventurers who went down into the dungeon's depths. But what did they face in that dungeon? How did they save the world?

Ah, that's what I hope you'll discover in this story.

For this is the story of YOU.

In the next volume, the party will challenge the dungeon once more, battle monsters to the death, and continue striving to reach that bottom floor.

I would love for you to stay with me to see how it all turns out.